LOLA KING

Queen of Broken Hearts

Stoneview Short Stories Book 1

First edition

Cover art by Outlined with Love Designs

This book was professionally typeset on Reedsy.
Find out more at reedsy.com

To my girl. We fell in love in October.

Love is like death, it must come to us all, but to each his own unique way and time, sometimes it will be avoided, but never can it be cheated, and never will it be forgotten.

Jacob Grimm

Contents

Foreword

Lots of Love,
Lola ♥

CHAPTER 1

we fell in love in october – girl in red

Rachel

Sometimes, I wonder if Rose White is even real. I watch her walk around school with her brother and their friends. I watch her long, jet black hair falling with slight curls all the way down to her hips. Her hair is thick, and she never ties it up. It's messy, like her twin's, Jake. I watch how gorgeous she is. Her tanned, Mediterranean skin, her long legs that make her look like a top model. And I wonder...is she real?

Often, her night blue eyes meet mine across a hallway or from opposite ends of a classroom, and she winks at me. I scoff and roll my eyes, always pretending I'm not affected by her constant flirting.

But I am.

I don't mean to be that kind of dramatic girl, but I think I always will be.

Rose isn't a one-time thing to *anyone*. She's eternal. Anybody who crosses her path falls in love with her, whether she wants it or not.

And she wants me.

She's always wanted me. I never tried to escape her, never truly. When we met, neither of us knew who we truly were. She was fourteen and I had just turned fifteen. Her and Jake had just moved to Stoneview, and all people would notice were the fading bruises on their arms.

They had been abused, clearly. And when we learned they were orphans and had just left one foster home for another, Stoneview kids assumed the headline of their story quickly: twins from abusive foster family are moved to rich town.

But I've always wanted to know more.

The Murrays became their legal guardians. That's Christopher Murray's parents, he's their foster brother now. Their best friend, their protector, always on their back, making sure they don't cause too much trouble. He's calm and collected, a quiet authority in exchange for the twins' chaotic personalities.

Jake and Rose are the center of everyone's world. At least at Stoneview Prep, our school. But I am an exception, Rose isn't the center of my world.

She became my *entire* world.

And as I watch her walk into Camila's house tonight – wearing a simple pair of black jeans and a loose white t-shirt tucked in them while everyone else is perfectly dressed in Halloween costumes – I wonder if my world will treat me as her sun tonight or leave me to the side with all her other satellites.

My best friend, Camila, rolls her eyes and turns to me as *Daddy AF* by Slayyyter comes on through the giant speakers in her living room.

I can't help the giggle that crosses my lips when I hear the

2

lyrics. Something about fucking models, popping bottles, and being a playboy in the Grotto.

Camila's voice cuts through the lyrics. "I swear someone put that song on on purpose," she huffs as she looks at Rose too.

Everyone looks at Rose when she walks into a room.

"Someone must have," I chuckle. The lyrics are just too perfect for her entrance.

I follow Rose walking across the room and toward the DJ booth, her head shaking with annoyance. That's the kind of house parties we have in Stoneview. Among the rich and famous, we always have DJ's at our parties. But the current one has been pushed to the side and Luke Baker took his spot.

Guess he's the one who put that song on. She reaches him quickly and gives him a slap at the back of the head before hitting a button to change the song as Luke is still laughing from his joke. Rose is taller than Luke and it always makes me smile. I love that she is taller than most people. Five-foot-ten of pure beauty.

Luke is one of Rose's closest friends. He was Chris Murray's best friend before the twins showed up. Since then, they all rule our school like the true kings they are.

Most people think I'm part of the 'lucky ones'. That's what some kids around us call their circle. Camila is our school's Queen Bee and she used to date Jake, hence me and her being part of the twins' inner circle.

Rose gets off the DJ booth with Luke and grabs a cigarette from the pack she was holding. I try to tell her to stop smoking, but she doesn't listen.

Rose White never listens to anyone but herself.

Her lacrosse friend, Ciara, hugs her hello and lingers a little too long. I shake my head and look away. It's always like that.

3

She was at my house a few hours ago, and yet I don't even know if we're going to talk tonight.

I'm not being jealous over nothing, Ciara is gay and she's been into Rose for as long as I can remember. She slept with her *once* and became yet another victim not being able to let go. I huff and turn to Camila as she offers me a flute of champagne.

"You look like you need it," she smiles.

"When did you go get this?" I ask, looking at the flute in my hand.

"While you were ogling your girlfriend." She raises an eyebrow, unimpressed.

"She's not my-"

"Yeah, yeah, I know how the Whilte family defines relationships. It was just to keep it simple."

Cam is...special.

To the world, she is the bitchiest, preppiest Queen Bee this town has ever known. She is mean, tough, rules with an iron fist, and does *not* accept mistakes from the people around her. Except Jake. She always accepts mistakes from Jake.

Our friend Beth suggested she should become part of the cheer squad once, the death stare she got almost annihilated her on the spot. Cheerleading is below her. Cam doesn't cheer for other people, she only cheers for herself.

If she lets you in, it's different. She lives under her family's pressure of being perfect. Her brothers are a disappointment, and she needs to keep up the Diaz family name. Her mom is a defense attorney and her dad a property developer. He made Stoneview what it is today. They're one of the most powerful families in this town and Camila has to live up to that. But her true self is kind and easily hurt.

She was the first one who knew about my sexual orientation,

and she never judged me for it. She let me confess to her about my fear of ever coming out to my parents, and she never pushed me to do it. I still haven't, but I know I would have her support if I ever did.

"Don't you think it's weird," my friend brings me out of my deep thoughts.

"What is?"

"That the twins just disappeared from their own birthday party yesterday. I mean, it's the biggest night of the year, and Rose and Chris didn't even show up to Luke's house for it. Then Luke and Jake stop by for five minutes and disappear?"

Yesterday, we had our Halloween ball at Stoneview Prep. It was meant to be a big night, because it was the 30th and at midnight, the twins were meant to blow out their candles. Their birthday is the main event of the year, and we always celebrate with a huge party at Luke Baker's house.

Strangely, they weren't even there. I left after thirty minutes, so I have no idea if the party carried on or not.

"What time did you leave?" I ask her.

"Ugh, Beth made me stay till late, but I was bored. I wanted to see Jake," she sighs.

My mouth twists. I feel sorry for her. Jake has never loved her the way she loves him. She's let him walk all over her for two years and now that they've finally had a clean breakup, she still hangs on to him.

"You know who wasn't there either?" she keeps going.

"Cam...don't do this to yourself."

"Jamie Williams."

"I know," I nod. "But it doesn't mean anything."

She snorts. "It means everything."

When Rose came to my house this afternoon she was restless

and angry, but I think she was scared too. She completely ignored the fact that it was her birthday. She didn't come to celebrate with me, she came because she wanted the safety of my arms. I think if her and all her friends weren't at the birthday celebration last night, it was for something more serious than just Jake wanting to see Jamie Williams.

"And he's not here tonight. I don't think he's coming. Neither will she."

"Chris isn't here," I reassure her. "It doesn't mean he's sleeping with Jamie, does it?"

"God, you're naïve, Rach."

"Cam, I love you and you deserve to be happy. Please, you need to forget about him."

"Like you forget about Rose every time she breaks up with you?"

My lips press together to avoid answering. Mine and Rose's relationship isn't the same as hers and Jake's. She doesn't want to see it, but I know it.

Or maybe I'm just as naïve as she is, blinded by love. I've got the White Syndrome. When your brain stops functioning because one of the White twins sets their eyes on you.

"BODY SHOTS!" someone shouts. I recognize Jason's voice and Camila raises an eyebrow. I guess our conversation is over.

"Beth is going to be delighted," she mumbles next to me. Beth is his fiancée.

"But you're still going to do one, right?"

She chuckles. "Well of course. You've got to give the people what they want, baby. Want to join?" She wiggles her eyebrows.

"You already know the answer to that."

I watch her walk away toward the long table in the middle of the living room where Beth is already lying down and pulling

6

her top up to show her belly button. Cam is so beautiful. Her gorgeous Latina skin, her curves, and especially her sexy ass, make most men drool after her. She has chocolate hair that she keeps just below her shoulders, and she was gifted with the most beautiful and rarest golden eyes I've ever seen. People say they're green, but they're not, they're pure gold.

I don't really want to participate in body shots. Cam and I became best friends through our parents when we shouldn't have. We are quite alike on the inside, but we show complete opposites to the world. I'm not the shy girl, but I am shy. I'm not an outcast, I always get invited, I participate in conversations and enjoy my time being part of Stoneview's finest, but none of it really makes me happy. The real me is well hidden, only Rose gets to see her. To the world, I'm always calm, rarely raise my voice. I don't engage in a conversation, but I will participate from the sideline every now and then. There, but not truly present.

It's never Rachel. It's Rachel, Camila's friend. Rachel, who hangs out with Beth and Camila. Rachel, she knows the twins. I don't mind being on the sideline. I don't mind being the sidekick. I don't mind being the quiet one who doesn't talk but observes.

Except when I hear...

Rachel, Rose's on and off girlfriend.

I hate being defined through Rose, even if everyone is defined through the twins.

It used to be Camila, Jake's girl. Now it's Camila, Jake's ex.

Jason, he fucks Rose from time to time.

Beth, that girl who hates Rose.

The latest one is Jamie. Jamie Williams, Jake's got his eyes set on her.

We're all just extensions of the twins. Or sometimes of Luke and Chris.

But I hate being Rose's on and off. And I know she knows despite me rarely mentioning it.

The only thing I get, that the other girls don't, is her promise that she will never cheat on me. And you know what? Yes, I am stupid enough to hang on to that. It just means that if she decides we're together, I get her complete attention. I get all her love, I get everything. But the downside is she will break up whenever she needs her dose of attention from the rest of the population.

For weeks I'll feel like I'm enough for her, and suddenly she will switch. She will go from my perfect girl to needing more. To be wanted by other people, to know that everyone still desires her more than anything they want in the world. She'll want to feel *needed*.

I told her that she should see a therapist. I mentioned that it was normal to need so much attention when she had been abandoned by her parents. But it goes deeper than that. Rose's head is a box of secrets, traumas, and nightmares that is sealed. Locked for no one to open and everyone to wonder about.

Instead of trying to get better, she prefers losing herself to Stoneview's typical debauchery. She prefers the hedonism of coke, threesomes, and expensive champagne. And on a calm day, she'll ease her mind with weed.

And me? Well, I'm just one of those drugs she doesn't have the strength to get rid of.

I decide to leave the main living room and head upstairs. There's a balcony at the back of the house that has a view of the Stoneview forest and a bit of the river that leads to the Silver Falls. I love it, it's my favorite spot in Cam's house. The Diaz are from the Dominican Republic, and they took years to build this Spanish style mansion. It's beautiful.

I open the double doors that lead to the beautiful balcony on the third floor and breathe in the night air as the wind ruffles my blonde hair. I've had two glasses of champagne and I feel tipsy. The cold air cools my head, but I still have a bubbly feeling deep inside of me.

I sit down on one of the loungers of the big balcony and look at the stars. I can hear the people partying in the backyard without being able to see them from here. So I decide to dream. Looking at the stars allows everyone to dream, right? I imagine a life where I'll get away from Stoneview with Rose. Far enough from my parents that I won't have to justify my choices.

Rose and I agree on the fact that we hate the concept of coming out. Why can't we just love who we love? Why do we have to conform to something so that we can be understood? At the end of the day, all I want is to share something strong with someone and it being reciprocated. I hate when I have to justify myself, to explain, to try and make someone understand. Either you know me enough to know every side of me, or you don't know me.

A dinner with your family, drinks with your friends, an event to defend that you are the way you are and to beg people to accept it? To feel validated in being different? Fuck that. Everyone's different. Everyday, every single person is different. Today I'm different from yesterday, and tomorrow I'll be a new me. So why bother explaining my sexuality to anyone? I don't need to be vindicated. I don't need others' approval.

Neither me nor Rose ever *came out* to anyone. We started dating, we broadened our horizons, we didn't fit into what society wanted from us. I've never been interested in men, and I never had a boyfriend. Maybe I'm a lesbian, maybe I'm bi.

9

Maybe I'm just in love with Rose. My parents think I'm just shy and they have these big plans for me and Conor McGill. Just another Stoneview kid whose rich parents are friends with mine.

They never really asked for my opinion. They still think Rose comes for friendly sleepovers and that she's a *really* good friend. How funny.

Why don't straight people ever have to come out as straight? Strange. I'd like a coming out letter from all my straight friends. *I'm sorry I'm different, I might be boring to you, sticking to what I've always been taught, but please accept me for who I am...I was born this way.*

I hear a slight movement behind me, and a hand suddenly wraps around my throat.

"Sunshine," Rose's raspy voice sing-songs in my ear. "Are you trying to light up the sky with all your beautiful thoughts?"

Her silhouette appears above mine, she's standing right behind the lounger I'm on and looking down at me.

Her hand isn't tight on my throat, a very light gesture of simply keeping it there to remind me that I'm not going anywhere until she decides so.

I chuckle at her stupid poetic words and shake my head.

"I was thinking of the concept of coming out of the closet."

She huffs, her hand leaves my throat, and she walks around, standing in front of me. "A stupid concept," she says.

Rose's voice is always hoarse. Like she's screamed too much or maybe because she has too many secrets that are dying to be let out and get squeezed down her throat.

In the night, her eyes look so dark, they're the same color as the sky. The stars reflect so deeply in them, I wonder if they come from her or the universe.

"Maybe it's a stupid concept to us because we don't have to go through the hardships lesbians went through decades ago?" I suggest. Hearing us call it stupid out loud brings other thoughts to my mind.

She nods, hearing me and genuinely thinking of my words. It's fascinating to converse with Rose. Never boring. She always listens and she always takes it further. She doesn't just nod and pushes it to the side. We can debate for hours, discuss topics that interest us and add to the other's opinion. We're passionate like that.

"Maybe they fought for us and went through hardships so we wouldn't have to worry about coming out and so we could allow ourselves to think of it as a stupid concept?"

"True," I nod. "Maybe we're a bit harsh when we call it *stupid*. I talked to that girl on Instagram. She thought I was completely wrong, she felt the need to come out to feel more comfortable around the people she loved. To be true to herself and the world. I guess it's...debatable."

"Everything is debatable amongst us gays. That's what happens when a whole group of people is still trying to fit into society under one category when everyone is unique and different."

I nod, looking at the beautiful woman standing above me.

"So you're talking to another girl, huh?"

I scoff a laugh. "Only in the comments of a post about coming out."

"Get up," she tells me as her cheeky half-smile spreads on one cheek.

I get up from the lounger and let her lie down. She grabs one of my hands and pulls me until I'm straddling her, a knee on each side of her. I wore her favorite dress today. It's a white summer dress with some tiny light blue flowers on it. I've put my own twist on it for Halloween but that thought was for her. She likes it because the flowers match my eyes. It's not the right time of the year, but it's her birthday so I put it on for her. I do look beautiful in it.

Her hands slide against my outer thighs, and I suck in a breath. She keeps pushing the dress up until her fingers can spread against my ass cheeks and she can knead them dutifully.

"What else were you thinking about? Your parents?" she asks quietly.

I nod. She knows if I'm thinking of the concept of coming out, I'm also thinking of my parents. My mind is half-focused on the conversation, and half on her fingers on me. They're slender and strong. She's so dexterous she could build my whole body with clay.

"Why?" she insists. "Did they say anything after I left today? Are you upset?"

She can be so caring. She always worries for me, she always wants me to be happy and safe.

That's because she's incredibly possessive.

If there's one thing Rose cannot stand, it's the possibility of the people she loves getting away from her.

It's a curse to be loved by Rose. Once she's got you, she'll never let you go, no matter how much *she* keeps flying free.

I shake my head. "They didn't say anything."

"So you're thinking of September, aren't you?"

She's too smart. She always remembers everything I tell her. She remembers everything she sees or hears. I've mentioned once, a few weeks ago, that I was worried about September. That my parents don't want me to go to college. They want me to do some pointless online course, get to know Conor over the summer and get engaged before the end of the year.

"What if I can't get away?" I murmur, too scared to voice it out loud. "What if...I just end up marrying Conor. Become a housewife like my mom. Have a couple kids, take care of him."

The thought makes me feel sick. The idea of having sex with Conor makes my insides twist and threaten to throw up my dinner. And giving birth to his kids...I shiver.

She chuckles lowly and shakes her head. "You know what's funny?" she says.

Her grip becomes tighter, and she brings me closer to her in a harsh movement, our hips crashing together. A zap of electricity courses from my clit to my heart, and the next beat sends lustful poison through my veins.

"That you think I would ever let Conor fucking McGill put his hands on you."

She sits up a little higher and brings her face down to my neck.

"Ah!" I cry out when her teeth meet my skin.

She nibbles and sucks until I'm completely writhing against her, dry humping against her black jeans. She gathers my shoulder-length hair in one hand and pulls until she has full access to my neck. Her teeth let go, move down slightly, and bite again.

"Rose," I whimper. "That hurts."

"Then why do you insist on pissing me off," she growls against my skin. Her other hand leaves my thigh to land on my panty-clad pussy. "Instead of focusing on Conor, why don't you focus on this." She pushes my panties to the side, strokes my folds and taps my clit a few times.

"That's a really wet pussy, Sunshine."

I nod, my breathing turning into pants. She keeps stroking my clit, taking her time, making me wetter by the second.

"Fuck," I moan, feeling my pussy tighten, the need to orgasm growing stronger.

The hand in my hair pulls and I let my head fall back.

"Make sure you scream loud when I make you come. I want Conor to hear you downstairs."

She doesn't accelerate, she doesn't slow down. She keeps her pace exactly the same, she only moves slightly as she gauges my reactions. But she keeps a torturously monotonous pace which somehow is too slow one second and too fast the next. So it's perfect. Perfect at making me want it badly.

When I grind or when I move, it breaks her rhythm and it's not good enough for me anymore. So I try to keep as still as possible, letting her stroke my clit over and over again.

My moans get louder, my breathing shortens, my thighs tense, and before I can take my next breath, I explode. I scream loudly, my lungs detonating notes of pleasure in the air as she keeps going, not changing anything as I ride out my orgasm.

"Enough...enough," I groan when she doesn't stop.

My clit is oversensitive, and I buck away from her. I grab her wrist with one hand and the other lands on the button of her jeans. Her fingers are slick with my juices, and she didn't even put them inside my pussy. I'm soaking for her.

I force her hand away from my pussy and put her fingers to her mouth. Her smile is carnal before she opens to let me push her own fingers in. I bring them in and out, making her suck my slickness as I unzip her jeans.

"Let's see how wet that little show just made you," I tell her, my breathing still ragged from the orgasm she gifted me.

My fingers slide under her sexy, black, silk thong and my breath hitches when I feel how wet she is.

"Oh, baby," I sigh in pleasure, my own body getting worked up again. "Why do you love making me come so much?" I stroke her clit and she shudders with pleasure.

"Fuck," she moans around her own fingers.

"Every bitch at this party is going to know I'm your favorite, Rose."

I insert one finger in her pussy while still making her suck her own. Her pussy squeezes me so tightly I'm not even sure I'll be able to insert another one.

"Shit," I moan, grinding myself against her leg. "Rose, you're so wet..."

I introduce another finger harshly, pushing past her tightness, and she whimpers against her hand. God, that sound. If I keep grinding against her leg, I'll be coming before she does.

I stop myself, let go of her wrist, letting her right arm fall back down, and move away until I'm in-between her legs rather than straddling her. I pull her jeans off her in a hurry, taking her thong with it, and throw them on the floor.

My hands go behind her knees and I push until her legs are spread and I have enough room to access her beautiful cunt.

I run my tongue from her asshole to her clit, taking my time to flatten it and she trembles with pleasure. "Just me, Rose. Tell me it's only me today."

"Yeah..." she rasps. "Only you, I promise."

I don't need anything else. I bury myself in her pussy, eating her out like our whole future depends on it. My teeth nibble at her clit and her legs tense under my grip.

"Rach..." she moans. "Aah..."

My tongue replaces my teeth and I devour her harshly, knowing she likes pressure rather than light strokes. Her moans are high and hoarse and I'm the one who shakes under them. I let one of her legs drop to my shoulder and bring my hand inside my panties. I stroke myself to the same rhythm as my tongue does her. I coat my fingers with my wetness before bringing them to her entrance.

I don't know why, it does something to me to mix our pleasures. I moan against her clit as I insert two fingers in her. She responds back when my voice trembles against her and she starts grinding against my face and my fingers.

I don't push deep in her, I stop just above her entrance, curl slightly, and make the motion of calling someone over. A 'come here' movement.

But what I'm really saying is,

Come here.

Come right now.

Come all over my face.

And she does. She comes so hard, my tongue has to lap her juices. She shudders against me, her back arching her pussy into my mouth.

I relish in her pleasure. I drop her other leg and rub my clit quick and hard, the opposite of what she did to me earlier. And when she screams my name loud into the night, I only need a few strokes to come undone.

This girl, she will be the end of me one day.

"Baby?" I whisper after a few minutes of silence.

My head is against her chest and her fingers tangled in my hair. Her breathing has settled, and she's stopped stroking my head. I wonder if she's fallen asleep, she does that a lot after sex.

"Mmh?" she intones sleepily.

I think I just woke her up.

"Were you sleeping?" I giggle.

"Nope," she lies groggily. "What's up?"

"You've got five minutes left of your birthday. Happy birthday."

I can't see her, but I can practically hear her smile as she tightens her right arm around me. "Thank you, Sunshine."

I love you, I don't say.

She knows it.

CHAPTER 2

beetlejuice chill – Life after Youth

Rose

"Look," Luke smiles as he shows me his phone.

There's a text from his new girlfriend, Emily Joly, saying she's coming to this party to see him. He's practically dancing on the spot.

I put a finger on his phone and scroll up slightly.

"I mean, you did insist about fifty times. That's practically harassment," I chuckle.

I lower my head on the bathroom counter and snort the line I just cut meticulously. Luke taps my shoulder and I come up before I can even finish. His cutting me off makes me choke slightly and I have to rub my nose about a million times.

"What?" I croak.

"I know we're upset about, you know, your older brother coming back from the dead and all that. But surely, even *you* know your next line is going to be borderline overdosing."

I huff and run a hand through my hair.

Yeah, this morning, the brother I shot three years ago came back to life.

Long. Fucking. Story.

What's important is he's alive, and he's going to try and get me and my twin back into his clutches.

"Are you officially taking over Chris' role when he doesn't attend a party?"

"Fuck no," he laughs before bending down and finishing the line I didn't.

I love Chris, he's more than a foster brother to me, but fuck if he can be annoying. He comes pretty high on the OFNR scale. I made it up especially for him and my twin, Jake. Overprotective For No Reason scale. Chris scores the highest anyone ever has. Jake is medium, Luke is the lowest.

My phone vibrates in my back pocket, but I don't look at it. It could be anyone at this point. Jake or Chris asking where I am. Some hookup wanting to, well, hook up.

Or it could be Nate. The dead older brother.

I shouldn't even own a phone, these things give me anxiety and I hate looking at mine.

All the coke I've done has hit me hard. I feel giddy, overconfident, *ecstatic*.

But most of all, my brain is busy and excited, meaning it can't focus on all the things it knows. That brain of mine is the bane of my life, and it takes careful fuckups to calm it down without killing it.

How am I meant to live everyday life with the stupid thing making constant lists of the things it remembers? And it remembers *everything*.

I'm a fucking genius who can't forget anything and it's a curse I can't get rid of.

Unless I'm on drugs.

Or fucking.

"Did you and Rachel fuck upstairs?" Luke asks deadpan. "Camila said you did."

I cackle a laugh and he raises an eyebrow. My tongue prickles in my mouth and I twist it around, taking my time to reply.

"I can't resist this girl," I admit. "I will forever fuck her anywhere and anytime I can."

He explodes laughing. "You've been at this party for like thirty minutes."

I pat his head and cock my head to the side. Luke isn't that much shorter than me, but I love making him feel like he is.

"Are you jealous because you couldn't keep me or because I fuck more than you do?"

We both laugh again. The ongoing joke of me and Luke not working out is a favorite in our group. It comes from losing our virginities to the other and it being the most disappointing three minutes of both our lives.

"I don't care," he pouts. "When Em gets here, it's game over."

"For you you mean. You do know your girlfriend is in love with me, right?"

He shakes his head, chuckling as he opens the bathroom door. "Okay, but seriously do you spike girls' drinks with a love potion or something?"

Back in the living room, we jump from group to group. Sometimes participating actively in conversation, sometimes hovering on the outside and only talking to each other.

The house has been decorated minutely with the scariest and most expensive decorations Camila could find. This year, the party theme is *Deadly Dolls.* Camila is dressed as Annabelle and I have to admit it's pretty sick and resemblant. Probably done by a professional makeup artist. That film was creepy as fuck.

Her house has turned into horror central. All her walls are covered in black cloth with UV red paint that imitates blood. One says, *I died right here,* and everyone seems to want to avoid the spot. There are hundreds of terrifying dolls hanging from the ceiling, pale and bloody. The food and drinks look like a tea party little girls have with their toys. Every time someone passes a doorway, bloody screams escape from some hidden speakers. In the hallways, there are children-looking creepy shadows and the laugh that escapes them is horrifying.

I love it.

The party, the conversations, the drugs...it's all keeping my mind away from real problems, and that's exactly what I needed tonight.

But there's one girl who always ends up wherever Luke and I are.

"He's not coming, Cam," I tell her with a condescending smile on my face.

I didn't have that many reasons to dislike the bitch before this year. Apart from that I get to choose who I like and there aren't many people I do like. Simple as that. I'm not particularly nice but everyone still wants to be my friend. That's because I'm pretty and because the guys and I are popular. Because Stoneview Prep has crowned us kings and we go with it.

But this year, Camila Diaz has started to seriously get on my nerves. She's not in love with my twin, she's obsessed with him. And she's starting to get dangerously heartbroken.

She loves him, and the dumbass fell for a girl he should have left alone. Jamie Williams is about a million times better than him and instead of accepting it, he keeps pushing, desperate to

21

make her give in.

I would bet my life they're both at home in his bed as I speak to Camila. But the bitch won't get the fucking hint. Earlier this year, I caught her and Beth bullying Jamie in the locker room, and I made a point to get them to stay away. I don't know how long it'll last though.

"I know," Camila offers me her most beautiful bitchy smile.

How can Rachel be friends with her? I simply don't get it. Is it a good deed or something? Charity maybe.

"He was with Jamie when I left the house," I tease her, but she doesn't say anything. No, the only thing that happens is that her perfect smile strains. "So, you know, stop following us everywhere."

"It's my house, Rose," she almost growls, but her smile is still there, barely wavering.

People are around and she doesn't want to be caught having an argument with me. It would be reputation suicide for her. "I can go wherever I want."

I think I'll forever wait for the perfect occasion to punch Camila. It'll come. Maybe one day she'll bitch about Rachel in front of me, or treat her like shit, and then I'll jump her, and it'll be pure satisfaction.

Speaking of, my eyes dart around the room looking for my sunshine. For that golden blonde hair and her beautiful summer dress.

She knows it's my favorite, she wore it for my birthday. She loves dressing up, but she still wore that summer dress for me, with her own Halloween twist on it. It's scary, just like she loves it.

People walk past, people dance, people drink and take drugs. But Rachel and her deliciously bloody outfit aren't anywhere to be found.

My gaze refocuses on Camila. She's been talking about something, but I really couldn't care less.

"Anyway, he's here, unlike Jake," she concludes.

No idea who she's talking about.

"Where's Rach?" I ask, ignoring what she just said.

This time, it's a wicked smile that spreads on her face. "I don't know," she shrugs, probably knowing exactly where she is. "Are you guys official or not at the moment? Because if you aren't, she could be anywhere. I saw her talking to Ciara earlier, now I can't seem to find either of them."

She pretends to look around for them and I roll my eyes.

As if.

As if Ciara would ever sleep with Rachel. She would die a thousand times before doing something that would get her on my wrong side. Because she still hopes one day, she can take Rachel's place. Being in love with someone makes you hope for crazy things, and Ciara is very much in love with me.

"Right," I smile, pretending to play her game. "Better go find her then."

"Or you could let Rachel do whatever she wants instead of being selfish."

"Are you seriously going all '*don't hurt my friend or else*' on me?" I gibe. "Please."

"I'm just saying, you and your twin have issues. You want everyone to be addicted to you while you still run free. It's psychotic."

I shrug. "Maybe we're psychos, what can I say." I move around her and step away from the little group we were in.

We're not psychos. There's only one White who is an absolute psychopath and he came back to life this morning. My older

23

brother Nate is a dangerous human being.

Hence why I had shot him in the heart.

It feels like it happened a lifetime ago. It's weird to think I missed a shot.

A shiver runs down my spine. Our ex foster parent taught me how to shoot. When I missed...

My brain fights my drugged-up state, starting to remember exactly how my life with Mateo Bianco used to be.

"No," I mumble to myself. It helps to order my brain out loud.

Still, it starts listing how many times I missed targets while learning. It lists the insults Bianco used to throw at me. And the pain...

I wince. Not because I'm remembering how bad it hurt, but because I can't fucking stop it.

I pat my pockets for that little pack of white powder.

Nope, Luke kept it.

"For fuck's sake," I whisper as I slip to a quieter hallway.

I need to find Roy or Carlo. Camila's older brothers became good friends when I became one of their favorite customers. They're everyone's main contact for drugs in Stoneview. And rich teenagers are suckers for coke.

A key.

That's all I need to shut my brain up. Just one key.

It'll be super quick, it'll be so helpful, it'll-.

I stop myself short when I open the door to the backyard and my eyes land on Jason. He stands right in front of me like he was about to come in as I was about to come out.

Or sex.

Sex will do.

"Rose," his drunk voice rings quietly in my busy brain.

"Bathroom," I mutter.

He shakes his head in a sad smile. "Using me so early in the night? That's unlike you."

I want to roll my eyes, but I also don't want to push him too hard.

"It's not like that," I attempt to justify myself. "I need you."

And I do.

But people tend to extend my words into the future with the hope that what I say tonight will be valid tomorrow.

It won't, but I do need him *right now*. I need him to shut my brain up.

I used to reject Jason's advances. He's meant to be engaged to Beth. I wasn't rejecting him because I'm a good person who didn't want him to cheat on his girlfriend. I rejected him because I couldn't be bothered with the drama.

Thankfully, Beth cheats on him on the regular with our calculus teacher. The drama is inevitable at this point, might as well enjoy myself.

Jason is beautiful, he has a big dick, and he loves fucking me. So why is he being annoying all of a sudden?

He takes the only step that separates us and cups my pussy so suddenly it makes me gasp. That'll shut my brain alright.

"What do I get in exchange for making you feel good, huh?" he smirks.

I grind against his hand and fist his shirt with both mine.

"A good fuck," I pant as he pushes harder.

"What about tomorrow? And the day after?"

"Come on," I huff. "You're taken. You're *engaged*."

He chuckles sarcastically and slides his other hand to my ass. "Maybe tonight I'll fuck you hard enough that tomorrow you'll remember me."

Probably not, I don't say.

Instead of taking me to the bathroom his eyes widen as he looks behind me, and he takes a step back releasing me completely.

There's only one fucker that scares everyone that way. And I mean *everyone.*

I turn around, only barely catching Jason's excuse to escape.

"Better not be here hoping you're going to talk to me," I spit at Sam.

The love/hate relationship I share with this guy should be a whole Netflix series. I grew up with him, spending my whole childhood persuaded that I was in love with him. Turns out I was just limited on people who cared about me, and I thought it was magical to have him as a protector. I thought him caring meant he loved me, so I loved him back.

I gave it my all.

Just to be turned down over and over again.

And yet, the fucker still won't let me go. He still looks after me, he still keeps me close, he still watches me from afar thinking I don't notice.

A never-ending cycle. I can't fucking take it.

After three years of not seeing him, he showed up like...like he missed me. And until today, he kept me on a fucking leash, blackmailing me into doing petty gang jobs for him. Because he threatened to go to the police, to tell them I murdered my brother.

Brother who turned out to be very much alive. And he knew that.

I'm done with Sam. I know I say that every morning, and by lunch I usually am answering his texts, but I'm for real this time.

I. Am. Done. With. Sam.

He approaches me slowly, making the hallway look narrower

with his big frame, making the ceiling look lower with his six-foot-five body that is hard as rock.

His black eyes are on me, desperately trying to suck at my soul. His black hair, his black tattoos covering his entire body... everything is black, contrasting with his pale skin.

The silence he's letting stretch between us as he gets closer is making me uneasy, but I keep a blank face. Sam is the king of silence. He's an observer, not a talker. And fuck is he observing me right now.

"Aren't you too old for this kind of party?" I pinch my lips right after I talk.

Shit. Now he's going to know I'm uncomfortable. I talked twice in a row, trying to cover for the silence he forced on us.

His small smile confirms my thoughts.

"Drop the attitude, Rose," he simply says.

It's four simple words, but his English accent makes it sound like an order from a God. Drop the attitude or else...

Or else I'll put you on your knees and fuck that dirty mouth.

Or else I'll show you how my cock can shut up that stupid brain of yours.

Or else... I shake my head.

Get your shit together, bitch.

Sam is like the monster under my bed. I should fear him, I should call for help when I feel him stir to life. Instead, all I want to do is put my feet to the floor and see if he grabs my ankles to drag me under.

"I don't have an attitude," I grumble in response.

That's about all I can manage.

But then he mocks me, and I remember why I hate him.

"You have the attitude of a twelve-year-old brat," his tone rises so he can pretend he's imitating me. "Ooh fuck the world,

27

everyone is against me, you can all fuck off."

I tighten my fist only slightly before flattening my hands against my jeans.

"I don't have an attitude," I repeat. "If anything, I don't tell enough people to fuck off. Or at least not the right ones. So be good and fuck off."

I walk past him without a look back, but it only takes him a split second to grab my wrist tightly.

"Sam-"

"We need to talk about this morning," he finally admits. Aka, the moment my older brother showed his not-so-dead fucking face.

I laugh, this situation is ridiculous. "We don't need to talk about *anything*. We're never going to talk again. That betrayal was the last one."

"Rose." His grip tightens but I don't show anything. He's going to have to try a little harder if he wants to hurt me, I've had worse, much worse.

My eyes dip down to where his hand meets my wrist, and I try my best not to shudder. I dig my dark blue eyes in his deep black ones.

If I'm not careful, he's going to swallow me whole.

"Are you okay?" he asks.

My sarcastic laugh doesn't faze him one bit.

"Oh, you just love fucking up my life and then checking up on me. That's your thing, isn't it? Gets you hard." I sneer.

He lets go of my arm, as if disappointed in both of us.

"Please, be careful," he says quietly.

"Please, die soon."

I walk back into Camila's living room, frustrated, horny, and with a brain still trying to fight me every step of the way. I need the one girl I know can heal me. The fix that *fixes* me.

My eyes scan for Rachel again and I feel my lips spreading into a predatory smile as I find her giggling with Ciara in a corner of the open plan kitchen.

Oh, so my little sunshine wants to be mischievous tonight. She wants me to prove that I won't let her escape me. She wants to push me to possess her.

It will be my pleasure. Truly.

CHAPTER 3

she calls me daddy – KiNG MALA

Rachel

"But you'd be so cute in a cheer outfit." Ciara smiles as she puts a strand of hair behind my shoulder.

I chuckle and rearrange my hair, as if she didn't put it the right way. Ciara is cute, but she doesn't understand I'm already too deep into someone else to have even an ounce of interest in her. She doesn't understand that only Rose is right for me, for what I need.

"It would be my worst nightmare," I contradict her. "Tight skort and tight tops. I hate that."

"Do you prefer flowery summer dresses?" she asks as her gaze runs from my head to toes and back up.

I nod and take another sip of my drink. How long will it take for Rose to notice I'm talking to one of the only other openly lesbians in our school?

It's not that I'm trying to make her jealous, it's just that I'm trying to show her how it feels to wonder if you're on someone's mind or not. To wonder if they're thinking of you tonight, or of someone else they can fuck.

Conor walks behind Ciara and my eyes cross with his piercing grey ones. He shakes his head, and his smile sends a shiver of disgust down my spine. He knows I'm gay, and he knows my parents have no idea. We used to be close as kids, we told each other everything. But as we grew up, he began loving the idea of my parents playing matchmakers with us. He also started loving the fact that I was against it way too much. Keeping my secret is a little game for him. He's cruel and selfish, and he believes sooner or later he'll have me.

What he doesn't realize is Rose would never let him.

"Fuck," Ciara says under her breath as her eyes go behind me. *Finally*, I think.

"She's gonna kill me, isn't she?" She laughs slightly, but she sounds scared.

I shrug my shoulders, pretending Rose and I aren't obsessed with each other.

A hand lands on my left shoulder as Rose settles on my right.

"Should we get some drinks?" Rose suggests. I risk a quick look toward her and her devilish smile tells me she's got things planned. So why drinks?

"Sure," Ciara replies naively. They spend enough time to-gether that Ciara should know Rose is up to something, but she doesn't seem to realize.

Rose scratches her nose quickly and I notice the irritation under it. Great, Rose on coke is restless and a little too brave.

Her hand on my shoulder slides to my hip and she moves me around easily, steering me toward the kitchen. Ciara is already a few steps ahead of us.

31

"Are you trying to make me jealous, Sunshine?" she slips in my ear.

I shake my head and pinch my lips, trying not to smile. I'm feeling playful, and so is she.

"I was merely trying to get your attention."

"You got it, baby. Unfortunately, you also got Ciara's attention. I'm sure you already know how that makes me feel."

My lips twitch again but I look at her with my most innocent eyes.

"Don't look at me like that," she chuckles. "You deserve what's coming to you."

My heart skips a beat, my pussy clenches, and I relish in her hand tightening around me. We pass people trying to get Rose's attention. She waves them away or ignores them, her entire being focused on me. Exactly what I wanted.

We close the door behind us as soon as we enter the kitchen. Only the heavy bass of the music makes it past the door. Ciara is looking at the bottles of alcohol on the kitchen island, some guys are chatting next to her.

Rose and I go to the other side of the island.

"What drink are you gonna make me?" Rose asks as she settles behind me. She wraps her arms around my waist, and I bend over to grab a bottle of whiskey, making sure to rub my ass against her.

"You like whiskey," I say lightly, aware that we have Ciara across us and those guys chilling not far.

"Can I have some too?" Ciara inquires. She sounds a little shyer than she was when talking to me alone. Now that Rose is here, she's retreated slightly.

I simply nod, pouring some whiskey in a solo cup and watching the amber liquid swirl. It's a little too expensive to be put in a red cup, but Camila isn't one to care about that.

I freeze.

One of Rose's hands just went from my waist to my right thigh. I pour way too much whiskey in Ciara's cup and her eyes widen.

"Whoa, I'm about to take a pill. I don't need to get that drunk."

"I-" I'm cut off by Rose's hand sliding up my thigh. I tense slightly when I feel it come under my dress and to the apex of my thigh.

Ciara is completely clueless to what is going on behind the kitchen island. We're standing, but the furniture is high enough that only our upper halves are showing.

Rose doesn't say anything. Behind me, she stays quiet and acts like nothing is happening at all. Her hand, however, comes to caress me very lightly through my panties. It's barely anything, but I shiver at her touch.

I scratch my throat and smile at Ciara. "Sorry, I'll make you another one."

"I'll take this one," Rose's throaty whisper comes up behind me.

I don't want to give it to her. She can get in such horrible states. I don't want another near overdose. The kind where she takes anything and everything. The kind where I'm always left wondering if it was a suicide attempt.

"You already drank too much," I reply. "And you took d-" Again, she doesn't let me talk. I seal my lips together when she grabs my panties from the front and brings her hand up, tightening them against my pussy so forcefully it almost hurts.

I gasp and it makes her chuckle lowly. I grab the bottle of Coke and pour some for Rose, then repeat the process for Ciara, my hands shaking. Rose is still keeping my panties high and tight around me, and it rubs against my clit as I bend over to pass her drink to Ciara.

"Thanks," Ciara says with a clueless smile.

I only nod a welcome, but Rose doesn't let me get away with it.

"Don't be rude, Rach," she says loudly. "Ciara said thanks."

Another twist of her hand and the lace panties I wore for her become too tight for me to stay quiet.

"Welcome," I almost shriek. There's a mix of pain and pleasure coursing through my body and I can feel myself reddening by the second.

If Ciara notices, she doesn't say anything. When the two other guys in the room come closer to her and make conversation, she turns their way, staying close but ignoring us.

"You wanted my attention, Sunshine?" Rose slips in my ear. "It's all yours."

"Rose." I release a shaky sigh. "We can't do this here."

"Ciara's gonna watch you come for me," she says with commanding words. They're a finality. "Remember that next time you try to make me jealous."

Her fingers release my panties, and she slides her hand between my burning skin and the material. There's a quiet hiss in my ear when she feels how wet she just made me.

"I want to lick your weeping pussy, baby," she whispers.

I barely manage to refrain a moan. Her words are fire, my pleasure melting for her. My clit is throbbing, and she purposely avoids it. My lips feel swollen as she rubs them and spreads them with two fingers.

Ciara turns to us, and it takes all my strength to plaster a blank mask on my face. There's nothing I can do about my blush though, nothing I can do about my knees wanting to bend. I grip the counter with both hands, desperate to ground myself.

"Remember, Rose?"

I have no idea what's just been said. I was too focused on Rose's middle finder tapping at my entrance, getting sucked in by the wetness of my desperate pussy.

But Rose has been following. She chuckles lightly and replies easily as she pushes against my back, keeping me trapped between the counter and her.

"Yeah, that was last Halloween. I tried to convince Ciara to come party on the North Shore with me. She wasn't quite up for it."

Ciara rolls her eyes, but a smile spreads on her face at the memory.

"Halloween is the most dangerous time of the year on the North Shore, you never know if the blood they're wearing is fake or not." She almost shudders saying that.

I try to breathe, I try to participate in the conversation, but Rose inserts a finger in my pussy so slowly, making it so torturously pleasurable, that I have to grip the counter tighter. My knuckles turn white as my breathing becomes more ragged. My body is burning from my toes to my pussy and all the way to my heart. I'm desperate for a breath of fresh air, desperate to scream with pleasure, but the embarrassment would be too great.

"Rachel?" Ciara's voice brings me back slightly. Rose's finger retreats just before she inserts another one.

"Wh-what?" I stutter.

Ciara's brows furrow with confusion as she looks at both me and Rose. Is she starting to figure it out? Oh my god, this is too humiliating.

And yet, I'm so wet I'm scared the sound of her fingering me, no matter how painfully slow, can be heard loudly.

"Ciara asked if you've been to a North Shore party," Rose insists, her mocking voice making the embarrassment unbearable.

For a second, I wonder if the two have planned this. To humiliate me publicly, to play with me like a well-strung instrument. Then I remember Rose would never share me that way. She would kill someone before they get to play with me like she does.

"Are you still with us?" Ciara waves her hand in front of me.

"N-," I scratch my dry throat. "No, I haven't."

My parents would decimate me if I put a foot on the North Shore of the Falls.

Ciara frowns again and her eyes lock with Rose's. "What are you doing?" she whispers as if she's finally in on the secret.

Damn it, she is, isn't she? She knows.

My eyes snap to where the boys are, only to find the spot empty. When did they leave? It's only the three of us in this kitchen now.

Shivers run up my spine, goosebumps cover my arms at the possibility of what could happen now that we're alone.

"Rose..." Ciara insists. "Are you...?" Her own breathing changes, it can't seem to keep calm as she slowly understands yet still not believing it.

"Am I what? Fucking my girl in front of you after you tried to snatch her?"

Her lips part in a small gasp as she struggles to take in a breath.

"Tell her, Rach, if I am," Rose tells me. I can hear the smug smile in her voice without having to turn around.

Ciara's gaze comes to meet mine, still questioning the reality of the situation.

Too embarrassed, I shake my head no. I'm doing it so quickly it makes the room spin. A mix of the pleasure and the blood rushing to my head making me dizzy.

But as soon as Rose notices I'm denying what's happening, she curls her fingers in me, the tips hitting the magic spot so tightly I shriek. "Yes! Fuck, yes she is!"

Ciara shakes her head, her own cheeks now burning bright. "I...I'll leave you two to it," she blurts out as she gets up from her stool clumsily.

I need to breathe. I'm so coiled up, I'm just desperate to snap. My heart is beating twice the rhythm Rose is moving inside me. I desperately clench around her two fingers and instead of accelerating like I silently beg her to. She stops.

The brutality of the halt makes me gasp with need. Her hand retreats from my underwear in no particular rush, her movements controlled and planned.

"Sit back down, Ciara," she orders darkly.

"What?" I try to turn around to read her face, but instead, I'm met with a strong hand between my shoulder blades as Rose forces me to bend over the counter.

"Rose!" I shout as my cheek meets the cold and sticky black marble.

Ciara's widened eyes meet mine as Rose's hand reaches my hair, tangling itself in it, and she pulls hard enough to make me wince. Rose keeps my head in place, forced to keep my gaze locked with Ciara's.

"Watch closely, Ciara," Rose tells her, a winning tone dripping from her voice. "Pull your dress up, Sunshine."

"Rose," I whine weakly. I'm not sure why.

Is it because I don't want Ciara to watch? Am I scared someone will know how weak I get when Rose touches me? Am I scared someone else will walk in? Don't I want the pleasure I know she will bring me?

37

"You heard me," she repeats without an ounce of kindness in her voice.

I comply, lifting my dress up until she has a full vision of my black lace thong.

"Now spread those gorgeous legs of yours."

I do.

With her free hand, she lowers my underwear until they're stretched around my trembling knees. The air feels cold against my dripping core. No matter how much I'm trying to keep still, my hips keep shifting, my sex desperate for friction.

Rose kneads my right cheek before her fingers reach my entrance from behind.

She taps lightly, slowly making her way toward my engorged clit. But as she gets closer and closer to it, she slows down and goes back to my entrance.

I groan loudly, a wordless complaint that comes from deep in my constricted chest and resonates loudly around the room. Ciara's eyes become hooded, and she shivers in her seat.

Rose's pad of her finger taps back to my clit slowly and she grazes it. My breath hitches, my lungs burn, my heart stops functioning as I wait to see if she will keep it there or back away.

"No," I mewl as she leaves my clit again.

"Do you want to play games with me, Sunshine? Do you want to flirt with Ciara and make me look for you? Or do you want to be mine and let me pleasure you?"

"I want you," I whine. "I want pleasure...please," I pant.

"Hear that, Ciara?"

"Rose...I...I didn't mean to-" But Ciara is cut off by my scream of pleasure as Rose finally unleashes on my clit. I cry out so loudly, I fear someone will come into the kitchen.

"Rose," I moan loudly. "Please...please don't stop."

38

She keeps going, roughly using three flat fingers to cover my whole clit and entering a fast rhythm of rubbing.

My heart drops in my stomach as my lower belly tightens to extremes I thought unimaginable. I need to come so badly I'm almost sobbing on the table knowing I'm almost there.

"Do you want me to make you come?" Rose's hoarse voice is the devil in my ear as she slows down her pace. "Do you want to come while Ciara watches?"

"Yes...yes please," I groan deeply. "Please, please, make me come."

She accelerates again, the pleasure coming back tenfold.

"Look at her," she growls low. "Look at her while you come all over my fingers like the desperate bitch you are."

My eyes snap open, locking with Ciara's. Her dilated, lustful pupils are probably matching mine as I explode in uncontrollable screams. My knees buckle but I'm held back by the hand in my hair, by the counter, and by Rose's fingers that suddenly bury themselves in my pussy violently. I scream harder at the intrusion and she fingerfucks me harshly. I writhe under her touch, I keep my eyes on Ciara, not wanting to get caught disobeying when I know following orders brings me pleasure. Ciara is panting, her hands gripping the counter tightly.

But Rose isn't nearly done. She rubs against my g-spot as her fingers tighten in my hair. I moan loudly, I buck my hips back and she straightens her two fingers, fucking me deeper.

"You're dripping. At this rate, you're gonna stain the kitchen floor. Dirty girl."

And I know she's right because I can feel the wetness trickling down. I can feel it at the apex of my thighs despite my spread legs. I can hear the obscene sound of my slickness as her palm slaps my pussy every time she fills me up.

I can't even reply to her, all I can do is attempt to breathe in-between the filthy moans that escape my mouth. She shifts her hand until her palm grinds against my raw clit as she fucks me harsher, and I buck against it.

"Do you really deserve another orgasm?" Rose asks me, the possessiveness still palpable in her voice.

I shake my head, completely taken in her game. "No," I whine. "No, I don't." Still, I grind against her hand, I push against her fingers to take them deeper inside me, my walls clenching around them.

I don't know what I hoped from my reply. Mercy? Her giving me an orgasm because I was honest?

"No." Her hand retreats brutally. "You don't." And her words are final. She takes a step back and away from me.

I know she's observing me, watching me tremble, watching me squirm with the need for pleasure. I can't move, beaten by my first orgasm and desperate for the second one. I was so close. It's like I'm satiated but incomplete. I tasted heaven just to be sent down to hell.

I hear Rose's boots walking around me until she appears in front of Ciara. Her friend gets up from her seat right away. She's trembling with need, her eyes wide and her pupils blackening her usually light eyes.

Rose's hand that was initially in my hair grabs Ciara by the jaw, forcing her to watch as she puts the fingers that were in my pussy in her own mouth. She's much taller than her friend, she towers over her with all the power she knows she holds. Rose sucks at her fingers, moaning at the taste I know she loves. The one that usually brings her to her knees. She licks them clean and makes sure to swallow every last drop.

Her voice is covered in lust when she talks to Ciara. "Show me your tongue."

Ciara's tongue darts out hesitantly before she licks her lips and then finally obeys. She sticks it out, presenting it as if waiting for an elixir from the gods.

Rose lowers her head, sticks her tongue out, and licks Ciara's tongue. It only lasts a second, she doesn't linger, and she doesn't let Ciara indulge in the pleasure.

When she straightens her head, she looks down at her friend, enjoying the desire on her twisted features.

"That's as close as you will ever get to taste her, Ciara. So I suggest you stop wasting your time." She releases her jaw and cocks her head to the side, in that condescending way she does so well. "Now run along."

Ciara doesn't even grab her cup, she runs out of the room without looking back.

Rose turns to me, and her smug smile shatters me.

"You can get up now," she says. I don't know if I was waiting for her to allow me to, or if I was too exhausted to, but I slowly straighten up and pull my panties back up. My breath has finally calmed but my heart is beating a little too fast still.

I walk on trembling legs as I round the kitchen island and join her.

"Let me make you feel good," I whisper. "I want to see you come."

Rose shakes her head. "No, you pissed me off. You don't get to see me come, and you don't get to come again. Not until I say so."

My lips spread into a sick smile, and I can tell she sees it by the way she so suddenly gulps.

"Wait until I get you home alone," I tell her with a gravelly voice, lust forcing my usually high notes to drop. "See how you

41

enjoy being a little smartass then."

Her eyes shine with need, but she still shrugs. "We'll see."

She leaves me behind, trembling and desperate for more of her.

CHAPTER 4

Danger – Jucee Froot

Rose

I don't know what's wrong. I don't know if it's because I've finally quieted down my brain or if it's the impending doom that has been following me since this morning, but I somehow don't feel safe in here.

I roll my shoulders back and stretch my neck as I down another glass of water. After desperately trying to shut down my mind, I'm now looking for some clarity as I try to follow Luke and Camila's conversation. I squint my eyes and look around. The smoke machine spreading fog all around the house has dried my contact lenses and it's giving me a headache. I love a good party but shit, tonight I can't focus. Not when I know my older brother is somewhere in Stoneview, waiting, biding his time, getting ready to pounce any minute.

What if he turns up here? Jake isn't here with me, Sam isn't on my side. Anything could happen.

Worst case scenario, I die. Can't be that bad.

"What?" Luke chokes as his head snaps toward me.

Beth is here with us, when did she join? I run a hand across my face, desperately trying to grasp what the fuck is happening.

"Rose, what did you just say?" my friend insists.

Maybe I talked about dying out loud. I must have because he's looking at me with his worried face. That's rare for Luke.

I shake my head at him and smile. "Nothing, I'm so fucked, I don't know what's happening."

"Too much weed to take down the high from the coke, that's what's happening," Luke explains. Looking at his palish face, I understand that he's feeling the same as I am.

I smile remembering parts of my night. I fucked Rachel in front of Ciara. That felt really fucking good. But the adrenaline from that and the high from the coke drove me a little insane, so I smoked with Luke. Too much. Always too much.

I'm gonna die from *too much* one day.

Excess and bad decisions put her here. That's what I'll have on my grave. I can't see the line that separates fun from excess. I always want more. There's always that cup I shouldn't have downed, that line, that puff. That girl I shouldn't have fucked.

If I could stop myself from crossing the line, Rachel and I would never need breaks, Chris would never look for me, Jake would never be mad, and I would save myself a lot of fucking headaches and hangovers.

I sigh and squeeze my eyes shut, trying to relieve some of the eye burn again.

"I need fresh air," I say before escaping toward the backyard.

I watch as some guy with a mask scares a girl from the Cheer team.

"Stop it, Ben," she scolds him as she hits his shoulder. "You know these stupid things scare me."

I look back ahead of me and keep going. I don't get what's so scary about masks, or Halloween. I love this season, and not just because I was born on the 31st of October. I love the fog in the early morning. I sit down by my window and watch it cover the backyard at the Murrays. It's calming, grounding, it keeps me out of my thoughts. I love the coziness of Fall.

But it's more than that. I am comfortable around things that make people uncomfortable. I don't get scared walking the haunted houses at the funfair, I don't fear people jumping at me, the blood, the masks, the clowns. People jump in fear and people are scared because deep down they're brought back to their instincts. They're scared to die.

And I'm not scared to die. I'm not scared of anything.

Except Mateo Bianco. And he always left me alone at that time of year.

When I was younger, I liked Fall because it's when the temperatures would start to drop, then it would be easier to hide the bruises Bianco left on my skin, and the cuts from the whippings. It meant less questions from the people around me.

Above all, Halloween meant Mateo would be gentler because of my birthday. Gentle Mateo was a rare occasion that I learned to cherish.

But all of this doesn't apply this year. Yesterday, I was meant to celebrate my birthday with my twin at midnight. Instead, I spent it with Sam on the North Shore, picking up packages and keeping people company while he was doing god knows what to people that pissed off his boss.

This year, I think I feel the same fear others do when they feel haunted. I'm finally starting to see Halloween as more than a night that gets me giddy and excited. This year, I'm scared. Because my older brother is back. He truly chose the right night to come back from the dead. And wherever Nate goes, Bianco isn't far.

I shudder, thinking about my ex-foster parent. I don't want him to find me. He's had three years to think about everything he'll do to me because I ran away from him. Fuck. Fuck, I know he's going to find us. Nate will tell him, he'll take him straight to us. To me.

I take a deep breath of cold air, stretch my neck, and sit on a garden bench next to a giant doll covered in fake spider webs. Stoneview forest, that sits at the edge of the Diaz estate, is right behind me and my back prickles with a bad feeling. I rub my eyes, the sting from my contacts really giving me a headache. I need Rachel. *Again.*

I told her she pissed me off, but I don't even remember why. That was hours ago. Now I want her next to me, I want to make her come again. I want to bury my face in her pussy and find peace.

My thoughts have been raging since this morning and there are only a few places I feel safe when I'm this way, one of them is between Rachel's legs. She's soft, she's beautiful, and she's mine.

All. Mine.

And I need something that's mine, I need something I can hold onto and that I know won't hurt me. Or at least not in ways I don't want. Rachel hurts me in the best way. It's cathartic.

Leaves ruffle behind me and I stiffen. Fuck, why am I so scared tonight? There's a raging party inside, people high on coke and ecstasy having fun. There are sexy girls dressed as slutty dolls and some as broken toys. And yet, I'm here, thinking of my forthcoming tragedy.

A branch cracks and I jump with surprise, turning around

straight away.

No one.

Shit, I'm going paranoid as fuck. Too much weed, *way* too much weed. I must be having a bad trip or something. I run a hand behind my neck and turn back around to face the house.

My heart drops twenty stories when I fall face to face with a shadow. I refrain a scream as my hand automatically grabs the doll next to me. It takes me a few seconds to realize it's only Rachel. She followed me out.

God, she can be so creepy, and she knows it.

My eyes run over her whole body. She is stunningly beautiful, and her outfit shows who she really is. With makeup, she turned herself into a horror doll. It's a reference to us, but no one knows that.

She has bloody tears pouring out of her eyes, that she has darkened with layers of black eyeshadow, and she is much paler than usual. She's wearing a red contact that contrasts with her other blue eye. She's put deep pink circles on her cheekbones, fake blood pours out of her lips, and she drew an on/off button on her temple. To complete the look, she's stuck a fake bloody knife against her collarbone.

"Why are you so jumpy?" she giggles.

My heartbeat slowly calms down, my ribcage doesn't feel constricted anymore. But I still feel like someone is watching me from somewhere behind me. The hairs on the back of my neck are raised, waiting for someone to pounce and grab me.

"Rose?" Rachel puts a hand on my one still tight around the arm of the giant porcelain doll. "Are you alright?"

I release the decoration next to me and smile at the beauty in front of me.

"I'm always alright when you're with me."

47

She smiles back, almost shyly, blushed from the compliment, and straddles me slowly. She puts her burning body against my cold one and wraps her arms around my neck.

Rachel often does that, putting her warmth against me. She's constantly burning, and I'm constantly cold. We fit together perfectly. The heat of her skin always brings my cold one back to life. The same way her warm heart wraps around my frozen one like a much-needed blanket.

I relax in her hold and wrap my arms around her waist, bringing her even closer than she already is. I hold her tightly, making sure she can't get away, making sure she's there to protect me against the ghosts watching behind us, against the phantom pain from my past.

I breathe in her chamomile and honey shampoo, I delight in her softness. God, she feels good. Her arms tighten around my neck, feeling my need for comfort. She doesn't know what's up, she never does, but she's always there for me. No matter what, she's always there.

My heart pinches, like every time she is perfect to me, and I'm reminded of how imperfect I am. Beauty broke me, intelligence cursed me, and now I'm left being a cold bitch to the rest of the world. And when I'm at my best, when I'm with Rachel and showing my better side, it's still not enough. It's too dark, too broken, too incomplete.

I wish she completed that broken side...but she doesn't. No one does. There aren't enough pussies on the planet, there aren't enough drugs, there isn't enough pain. I will forever search for completion. I will always search for what Bianco stole from me.

But I will never find it.

"Your perfume has faded, you smell good," Rachel whispers in my hair.

Her words make me chuckle and I feel it resonate in her chest. "You really hate that perfume, don't you?"

"It doesn't suit you."

I'm surrounded by the freshness and softness of her scent while she's probably surrounded by a mix of cigarettes and alcohol. But I know she likes it.

She likes my grittiness and my roughness. She likes my hoarse voice, my sarcasm, my tattoos, and my bitchiness. And she likes the smell of whiskey and cigarettes. The thing she doesn't like is my flowery, girly perfume that smells of lilac, violet, and geranium. It's too prim and proper. It reminds her of Stoneview, of her parents. Rachel Harris wants rebellion and emancipation. She wants a taste of freedom.

Don't we all?

"Hey, do you want to go home?" she asks, her head still buried in my thick, black hair. She takes a deep breath, as if making sure she gets enough of me before we separate.

"Yeah," I murmur back. "Let's go to mine, I'll drive us."

"You're too intoxicated to drive," she says louder. She pulls away from me and breaks the bubble of safety she had put us in. "I'll call my driver."

Both our features twist at her words. "That sounded so shit," she admits.

"So Stoneview," I smile. "But I guess using your homophobic parents' money to go back to your girlfriend's house and get fucked is a good way to get back at them."

Her laugh lights up the stars above us, and she rests her forehead on mine. "That sounds about right. I'll go get my phone inside. Meet me at the front in five."

I let her go and watch her walk across the backyard to make her way inside. I slowly get up, feeling slightly better than I was

49

before she found me.

And yet, I can't help but turn back toward the forest. Someone was watching me, watching us, and I know it. I almost want to call for them to come out of hiding but I don't want to sound insane. Maybe I am? I squint my eyes at the dark space, at the trees that seem ready to swallow me whole. The wind ruffles the leaves, an owl hoots into the night. Apart from that, nothing.

I shrug, turn back around, and walk back toward the house.

I cross the living room barely paying attention to anything going on. I'm about to reach the foyer when I hear Rachel's awkward laugh. I look around, scanning the people around me. She must be close if I can hear her over the music.

"The fuck?" I mumble when I see her standing next to a guy about twice her size. He's got an arm around her shoulders, and I know he must be hitting on her from the way her body twists with disgust. Still, she politely laughs at his no doubt macho jokes.

It only takes a split second for anger to start boiling my blood.

I'm on the guy in two long strides. Rachel sees me first, her eyes widening. She shakes her head at me.

"Rose-"

She's cut off when I pull at the guy's shoulder with a violence he didn't expect. He stumbles back and turns around to face me.

"What the fuck?!"

It's not often that people are taller than me, but shit this guy is a giant. I don't care though. The adrenaline coursing through my veins brings back the high and braveness from the coke. I rub my nose, a reflex more than a need at this point.

"Rose, it's okay. Please let's go," Rachel pleads as she puts a hand on my arm.

I ignore her and shrug her off. I'm focused on him right now.

"You alright, big guy? Need any help hitting on a girl not interested in you?"

He laughs condescendingly and gets in my private space, towering over me and making me smile at how pathetic he is.

"She never said she wasn't interested."

"Then maybe you need to learn how to read the signs."

"Who the fuck are you? The cockblocking best friend? Your bestie didn't push me away. She was enjoying herself."

It's my turn to laugh. "I get it, sometimes it's hard to understand not everything is about your cock and it being blocked. You only speak big, strong, manly language, don't you? Let me adapt to your level." I'm vaguely aware of the people gathering around us, of the flash of Beth's phone filming me on my right, but fuck if this dickhead thinks he's going to win this one, he's got another thing coming.

I get closer to him, pushing against him this time, looking up into his eyes and keeping what I know is my psychopathic smile on. "Put a hand on my girl again and I'll make you swallow your own balls, asshole." My smile drops at the same time as he realizes I'm not to be fucked with.

I'm not an athletic girl, I don't have big muscles to show my strengths. I'm actually skinny, practically underweight. People know though, they see it in my eyes. The danger, the hidden strength that hides inside people that were forced to take on too much shit in their lives. The tension that stretches between us only lasts while he hesitates if he wants to get in a fight with me or not.

He chooses being a typical asshole instead. The kind that meets a lesbian couple and assumes we're only here for his entertainment. The kind that assumes his dick is the center of everyone's world.

"Shit." He turns to Rachel slightly. "You should have said you were into pussies, sweetheart," he says to her. "I would have invited your girlfriend into the conversation earlier. Because I'm sure I can change your mind."

Sweetheart.

He called her, *sweetheart.*

Time stops for a few seconds. He says something else but the fury in me is already making me deaf. It's making my vision monochrome too. All I see is thick, bloody, *red.*

"Oh no..." I vaguely hear Rachel. She huffs but doesn't try to stop me. If anything, she's mocking him. "If only you hadn't called me sweetheart."

I chuckle so darkly, the guy takes a step back. But it's too late for him. I pounce on him and he tumbles back with surprise. My fist is about to land against his temple when two hands grab me.

"No, no, no," a voice I recognize too well speaks to me.

"Let me go, Carlo," I growl.

Camila's older brother is strong. Too strong for me to get out of his hold when he holds me from the back.

"Let me fuck him up!" I shout with fury.

"He didn't mean to bother. Right, Chad?" Carlo says to the guy.

Fucking *Chad.*

"Fucking hell, fine I didn't mean to hit on your girl. Chill the fuck out."

"We were just leaving," Rachel jumps in. She puts a hand on Carlo, silently telling him to let me go.

"I'm not kicking you out," he replies. "But promise you're not fighting anyone," he insists as he puts me down.

"I'm fucking leaving," I growl as I turn to him. "I would be gone already if that dick on legs wouldn't have made Rach feel so fucking uncomfortable."

"Damn, I said I was sorry," the idiot exclaims behind.

"Enough," Carlo tells him. "Rose, you can't just-"

"Bye," I ignore him as I take Rachel's hand. I'm not about to debate with two men. Lord only knows where it leads us ladies.

"Miss Harris, how was your evening?" Rachel's driver says as he opens the backdoor of the black town car for her.

"It was good, thanks Marc."

She is polite to him, but she never makes conversation despite his kindness. He never judges her, never judges us. He keeps quiet, doesn't spill anything he sees. My kind of guy, really. But Rach hates everything that has to do with her parents, that includes Marc.

She waits until the window between him and us is raised before she grabs my hand.

"I like Halloween," she tells me. "It's for the weirdos and the fun people. Like us."

"We're not weird, Sunshine." It's always like that, she's been told so many times that anyone who falls under the LGBTQ+ umbrella isn't *normal* that she still thinks she isn't. That what we're doing is wrong. She's accepted it, but she's accepted herself as abnormal.

I just want to take her out of Stoneview. I want us to go to college and discover the world outside of a luxurious, only barely open-minded town. Stoneview elected a female, African American mayor and thought they did about as much as they could in the name of feminism, diversity, and anti-racism.

"You know what I mean," she insists. "I'm just saying, everyone puts on a disguise on Halloween." She shrugs. "I just let my mask fall."

My gaze runs across her bloody outfit.

"A knife and a lot of blood. Is that what happens when you drop your mask, Sunshine?"

I circle the back of her hand with my thumb to keep her calm. Beneath Rachel's angelic appearance, there is a demon hiding. A majestic spirit that craves blood and pain. That's my favorite thing about her. She hides it so well, it's buried so deep, that when it does come out, it's lethal, raw...*orgasmic.*

"Yeah," she murmurs back. "That's what happens."

I smirk and shift so my left leg meets her right. I twist and put a hand on her thigh.

"I'm gonna make you come again."

"Here?" she scoffs. "Absolutely no way."

My eyes lock with hers and it takes a few seconds before she understands that I meant my words.

"Rose," she says in a low warning. "No."

I bite my lower lip and nod as my hands slip underneath her dress. "Yes."

I grab her panties with both hands and drag them down as I get on my knees in front of her.

"My, my," she whispers, now scared that Marc could hear us. "Rose White on her knees for me."

"Anytime, baby."

She's smiling until I bare my teeth carnally. "I'm going to devour you. I'm going to bring you to the brink of sanity. I'm going to spell *crazy* with my tongue and paint you with your own slickness."

"Fuck," she sighs with pleasure before I even touch her. I grab the back of her knees and drag her in one violent movement until her ass is on the edge of the seat.

"Sunshine...why are you so wet? I haven't touched you yet."

"Because," she pants. "Your tongue is as lethal with your words as it is when it touches me."

I look up so she can see my smirk. "I know."

"Your voice, Rose. It does things to me."

And for her enjoyment, I let it drop a few octaves before talking again. "I know. Now let's hear yours."

Before she can realize, I disappear beneath her dress and lick her all the way from her anus to her clit.

She tastes like heaven. Like an angel dropped a tear on her pussy and turned it into a fountain of pleasure. Her slickness wakes up my tastebuds, making my whole body aware that it's time to enjoy its favorite taste.

I lick all around her needy bud, making sure to avoid it as much as possible.

"Rose," she whines as she squirms.

She drags her dress up, uncovering my head and grabs my hair tightly, making me hiss in the process.

"You've teased me enough tonight," she rasps. It makes me chuckle and I watch in worship as her entrance tightens under the pleasure.

Licking her wetness from my lips, my lower belly twists with anticipation. Her smell is divine, and I want to drown myself in her. She doesn't let me tease her any longer. She tightens her hold and bucks toward my face.

Her moan resonates loudly in the car as she starts grinding against my tongue. I try to harden it and slide it inside her pussy, but she changes directions. My lips, my nose, I'm completely immersed in her. She shamelessly grinds her hips, getting the pleasure she needs from me, and I drink her up like I just spent days in the desert.

My hands shoot to her ass cheeks, and I lift her up slightly, bringing her even closer. My own pussy is dripping, my underwear sticking to me, but I don't stop devouring her. I'm out of breath, my lungs burning. I'm choking on her and it's the happiest death I could hope for. Her screams are the essence of my happiness and my stomach tenses with pleasure every single time. But I don't touch myself.

Instead, I tease myself, grinding against my own jeans. Selflessly, she tries to back away to let me breathe, but I don't let her. I nibble her clit between my teeth and force her against my face. I don't want to breathe, I only want her. I want my life to end between her legs. I'm fucking possessed when I groan into her. Taking my time, I bring a hand to her entrance and enter her with my middle and ring fingers. I curl them slowly but with force. At the same time as I take her clit in my mouth, I caress her g-spot.

She explodes.

She drenches my face as she screams my name, and still, she keeps grinding against my mouth.

If Marc didn't hear that, he was already deaf. If not, she probably destroyed his eardrums.

My jaw hurts and black spots are dotting my vision, but I don't let her go when she tries to pull away.

"Rose! I can't!" she screams in pain.

Shit I want to die like this, doesn't she get it? My tongue burns, my whole body is trembling with need for air, but I want more of her.

"Please...please..." she cries out. "No more..."

But if she doesn't want more...why does she come so hard when I press my thumb against her clit and lick her entrance? Her shaking thighs clamp around my head and the second orgasm crashes through her in waves that resonate through my own clit.

She rides it out until she can't move anymore, and when she falls slack against the seat, panting and mewling, I finally pull away.

I take a huge breath of air as I fall backward, and my neck hits the seats just below the window that separates us from Marc.

"You're insane," she breathes out as she lazily gets off from her seat and slides to the floor.

She crawls on top of me, straddling me, and pushes her delicious lips against my wet ones. She licks my lips, my cheeks, nibbles at my chin. She pushes her tongue into my mouth despite knowing I need to catch my breath. She licks the inside of my mouth, tasting herself, clashing teeth. She eats me out like I just did to her pussy, and I'm so coiled with pleasure I can't help but grind against her.

She puts a hand between us, rubbing her knuckles between my legs. She pushes the hardness of my jeans against my clit, and I groan with need.

"Do you want to come?" she asks.

"Fuck," I suck in a breath. "Yeah..."

She smiles, her eyes lighting up with lust, and kisses me again. She rubs me through my jeans, painfully and deliciously. I feel my whole body tensing up, my legs start to shake as it becomes more difficult to inhale.

"Fuck...fuck...Rach..." I pant, my voice getting higher every time I try to push a word past my lips.

"You're so beautiful," Rachel says. "Rose, you're so gorgeous when you're about to come for me."

The car suddenly comes to a stop, and we hear Marc's door open and close.

"*Shit!*" Rachel panics. She jumps off me just as I'm about to come. I can barely process what's happening as she pulls me up and sits me down on the backseat. She grabs her panties on the floor and bunches them up in her fist.

I groan a wordless complaint, feeling drugged up and tense, as Marc opens the door.

"We're here, Miss Harris," he smiles politely. He hands Rachel a sleepover bag with cheeks slightly flushed. He heard us, no doubt. Or at least he heard Rach scream my name. It was beautiful, I hope he knows how lucky he is.

He knows the code to get into the Murrays' estate, and he drove all the way up the hill, dropping us off right by the entrance. But we don't walk through the double wooden doors that lead to the main house.

Instead, I grab Rach's hand and drag her to the side of the house to access the backyard. I'm practically running across the lawn as I make my way to the pool house. That's where my brother and I live. The Murrays love us like we are their kids, but they've always accepted that we need our own space.

I pull Rachel with insane need as I open the door to our small space. The entrance is a simple living space with a sofa, a tv on the wall, and a breakfast bar that separates the living room from the small kitchen. But never mind the fucking living room. I take my sunshine behind the sofa and toward the only hallway in here. It's short and there are two bedrooms on either wall, one last door at the end leads to the shared bathroom. Left is my twin's room. Right is where I'm taking my girl to fuck her until she sees stars.

"Is Jake here?" Rachel murmurs quietly as I push my door open and drag her with me.

"Since Jamie Williams' clothes are on our sofa, I'm going to guess yes."

"Jamie Williams? So they're together now?" Rachel says with surprise as she closes the door.

I want to reply, but her voice has become a dull sound. My eyes can't leave her hand holding the handle. I watch closely as the door meets the frame. It's like slow motion, my brain can only focus on that, on the motion it makes, on the little click as it falls into place.

"Rose, I'm here," Rach whispers softly as she starts walking toward me. "We close the door when I'm here, remember?"

I feel her soft hands on my cheeks, and she forces my gaze to defocus from an imaginary spot on the door and focus on her instead. I find the maya blue in her contactless eye and a weight lifts off my chest.

"You can talk to me," she reassures me. Because she doesn't know, and she doesn't understand why I get like this.

Like every time she wants to know more, I change the subject. "Fuck me."

She stays still for a short moment, maybe waiting to see if I'll regret pushing her away and finally share my past with her. When she understands it still won't happen, she relaxes and slides a hand along my neck, my collarbone and stops at my breasts.

"I'll fuck you," she admits shamelessly. "*My* way."

It only takes the way she pronounces '*my*' to wake up a sick need inside of me.

"Yeah?" she insists.

"Fuck, yes."

She smiles but her sweetness is all gone. With that blood on her face, her fake paleness and those big doll eyes looking at me, she's terrifying.

Terrifying and irresistible.

"And you're going to be good and take it all, yes?"

I nod, incapable of talking now that I know she's about to show her true self.

"Mm," she moans as she bites her lips. "I hope you don't die."

"I hope I do," I rasp.

She shakes her head slowly. "Well how am I meant to have fun if you do? Who am I going to hurt? You don't want me to play with someone else, do you?"

She closes the small space that was separating us and wraps a hand around my throat. "Do you, Doll?"

"No, just me."

"Just you," she smirks devilishly. "Get on the bed."

I jump into action. I'm so ready for this, so ready for her. So ready for the *pain*.

CHAPTER 5

Animal – AG, MOONZz

Rose

Rachel watches me as I sit on the end of the mattress in my underwear. Our eyes are locked as I slowly make my way backward. My hands slide against the sheets, my feet push me until I'm sitting against the headboard. Her eyes don't leave me, her smile getting more demonic by the second. A shiver runs through my whole body, waves of need tensing my stomach and tingling down to my clit.

"You're all strung up, aren't you?" she says in her crystal voice. "My little doll didn't come in the car, she was so desperate to."

My breath hitches when she opens the end-of-bed bench and grabs something in there. I already know what it is, but my eyes still widen when she pulls out a sharp kitchen knife. *Her* knife.

Lord have mercy on our souls, Rachel and I are made of pure sins. We're made of evil, we're irredeemable.

She peels off the prop knife she had stuck to her collarbone and meticulously places it on the floor.

"Time to play with real toys," she smirks when she straightens up.

She takes her time stalking toward me. She walks to the side of the bed and puts the pointy end of the knife against the pad of her index finger as she stops by my side, thinking where she's going to start her torture.

Slowly, she brings the knife to my collarbone and slides it between my bra strap and my skin. She's skilled, quick, and efficient. Before I can register the tearing, she's got my bra in pieces. I groan and shift with pleasurable tension as she drags the bits of clothing away from my breasts using the knife. Fuck, I just want her to touch me. I just want her lips on mine, her fingers in me. Is she going to put on the strap-on?

"Don't move," she growls low as she grabs one of my legs and pulls it toward her. She comes onto the bed and places herself between my shaking thighs. She runs the flat side of the blade against my abdomen, and then my groin, letting it slide against the silky material.

Did I wear silk panties hoping she would play this way tonight? Hoping her knife would slide easily against the material? Absolutely. But I'm never sure, Rachel rarely lets that side of her take over.

She holds the handle tightly and raises her favorite toy. She points it toward my mound, as if about to stab me, and just barely touches me with the point. Silently, she brings her free hand toward my covered pussy. She traces her thumb against my clit, and I gasp at the rush of pleasure. My hips buck up on their own accord and I wince when I feel the pressure of the blade against me.

She giggles like a horror film possessed kid, and goosebumps erupt all over my skin. "Don't move, Doll, you're going to get hurt."

"Not fair," I groan as I force myself to stay flat against the mattress.

She touches me again, pressing her thumb onto my clit and raising her finger fully knowing my body will rise from the bed in a desperate need to follow the pleasure. The point of the knife digs into me again, rushing adrenaline through my veins, and I moan when I reach her finger. I moan at the pain and the pleasure that mix together so well. She presses her thumb harder, she presses the knife further, and I feel it slowly piercing through my panties.

She takes her hand away, my body falls slack against the bed, and the pressure of the knife disappears.

"If you press against that knife again, you're going to bleed. You're going to be a bleeding little doll. How unfortunate would that be?"

She looks up at me, her eyes feral. The red contact, while scary, hides who she truly is. But the blue is terrifying, it shows the demons tainting her soul.

She doesn't give me time to reply, she grazes my clit harder and lifts her thumb again. And like the desperate bitch I am, I follow up, I let the knife dig into my skin, I let it puncture me until a drop of blood escapes. I moan loudly as her thumb brings pleasure to help with the pain. I grind against her finger and my panties soak up the drops of blood and my wetness.

She retreats her hand suddenly, making me groan.

"Enough, Doll. You're going to hurt yourself." She shifts, drops her head between my legs and extends her arm until she can rest the blade against my throat. "Stay still."

I push my head against the pillow, fear forcing my instincts back to life. But when Rachel bites the small cut through my panties, when she starts sucking at the material making me wish it was my clit. I fucking lose it.

"Rach," I moan as I squirm. I bring a hand to her hair and the other to the hem of my underwear. "Take them off," I beg desperately.

Her only response is pushing the knife tighter against my throat. Then she looks up and, fuck, the sight of her makes my whole body tremble. "Keep your hands to the side, Doll."

She goes back down, brings the knife with her and slices my thong in one quick movement. I jump with fear, then I'm forced to still when she puts the blade against my inner thigh. She goes up and down, up and down, making me shiver and apprehend her next move.

"Where am I going to cut you?" Her sweet voice is completely gone, replaced by lust and need for pain. "Here?" she says as she puts the point of the blade toward my knee. It disappears and reappears a little higher. "Here?" I let out a sigh when she licks the place it had touched before at the same time as she presses into my thigh. But she doesn't cut me.

"Or here..."

She presses at the apex of my thigh, and I can't stop the whimper that crosses my lips.

"There it is," she smirks at the sound that escaped me. "I want more of that."

I can't breathe, I can't move. My whole being is focused on her, focused on the knife against my femoral artery, on the pulse of my heart against the blade.

"Rachel..." I squeak in a whisper. This could be my time, this could be the end. Thrill runs through my veins, an excitement that nothing else can bring me.

"Are you scared?" she mocks me.

"Y-yeah," I pant, trying to hold my breath and desperate to let it all out.

"Poor little doll, she's so *so* scared," she giggles.

"Rach...shit...careful."

She drags the blade against my mound, my belly button, and stops at my breasts. I've always had small breasts, nonexistent might be more appropriate, but shit they feel very present now that I've got a knife going from one nipple to the other.

She uses the flat of the blade to tap against my hardened nipple and pinches the other one. She rolls it between her fingers, forcing moans out of my mouth before she lowers her head and grabs my tit between her teeth. I hiss at the pain, and she licks me better. I can't stop my hips from moving, from desperately trying to grind against something.

She lifts her head, and her eyes light up as she smiles. "Here," she concludes, pointing just above my nipple.

I shake my head in fear. "That's fucked-" I'm cut off when she cuts the thin skin just above my left nipple. I know it's impossible, but I almost hear the skin break. Inside my head, it's a dull *crack* as it tears.

"You should pierce those beautiful nipples," she says in a gravelly voice. "I want to be there when you do it. I *want* to do it myself." She sounds needy, bratty.

I tense up right away and it makes her laugh. "Not *now*. Silly little doll."

I don't have time to react, she drops her head to my breast again and licks the wound she just made. She bites above it and I feel more drops rolling out of the cut. It's not much, it never is, but to her it's like Christmas morning. And to me? It's fulfilling the ultimate need to be with someone I trust when I receive pain. It's the crucial point my brain needs to focus on.

She alternates between licking drops of blood and nibbling at my nipple, making me writhe with pleasure.

"Touch me," I try to order, but she's quick to bite me hard.

"Ow, Rach!" I whimper. It only makes her smile.

She pulls away and smiles at me. My blood has mixed with the fake one she had put on her lips and chin. She's beautifully monstrous.

She kisses my stomach, licks her way to my pussy, and the need for release builds up in me. She still hasn't even touched my clit.

But when she does, when she finally parts my lips, and her bloody tongue makes it to my swollen bud, I scream with pleasure.

She uses the occasion to cut me just below my belly button.

"More," I whine, when she slows down.

"Anything for my doll," she whispers against my clit. She brings the knife between my legs and sits back.

CHAPTER 6

Welcome to the Jungle – Tommee Profitt

Rachel

There's a darkness in me. I've felt it since I was a child. I've always known it was there. When I was little, my worried parents took me to see a psychiatrist. Their only response was that some children are *born* with evil in them. They took a guilt off my parents' shoulders. For a long time I thought, *where the hell did they get their degree from?* Until I realized they were right.

Like possessed children in horror movies, and Halloween scary stories. I have something in me that I'm constantly battling and suppressing. Halloween is my favorite time of the year, all the blood, all that gore, it makes me horny. It's not the fear, it's the darkness. It's the forbidden. It's the weird and rejected. My parents used to freak out when they found me in the living room at 3am watching horror films. At first, they thought I was sleepwalking. Sure, if it can make them feel better.

I wasn't. Since being a kid, it was a passion of mine to watch bloody scenes. I remember the peace that overtook me when I did that.

I've had an easy life, my parents are rich, they've always spoiled me. I've never needed anything, I've always had food on the table, Christmas presents, and anything I've ever wanted. I've never been traumatized by anything, and I wasn't assaulted as a child. I'm just *fucked. Up.*

The only problem I have with my parents is that they're homophobic piece of shits. I will never change them and they'll never know I'm gay. Never.

I am the way that I am because I was born bad. Nothing and no one put it in me. There is something inside me that needs to cause pain to people. There is a demon that can only be fed with blood.

Rose, there is something inside her that needs pain. I don't know why, but it's there. I can only assume it is because of her past. That secret past that never gets out of her head.

So we match. We match like fire and gasoline. We're explosive, dangerous, *hypnotizing.* And when a girl as strong and beautiful as Rose White gives you her body and her mind to play with. When she gives you carte blanche to feed her craving for pain. That's something no one would ever have the strength to refuse.

When I watch her like this, in a space between pain and pleasure, in a place of passion, coiled up like a steel spring, waiting for any sort of release...it's majestic. She's a Goddess that allowed me into her temple and I'm here to worship at her altar.

Blood is running onto her usual dark pink nipple. Her beautiful Mediterranean tanned skin is covered from belly button to pussy in her own blood. Apart from her breast, the cuts are not bleeding anymore. They're superficial and that's how I like them. I like having to push at her skin and bite at it to drag more blood out. I like when she thinks it's over and I reopen her wound with my teeth.

I've spread some of her own blood onto her clit and it looks beautiful. She's a work of art.

"Rach, please," she pants. She squirms with need and her hands at her sides tightly grab the sheets. She needs to come so badly right now, it's quite a sight.

"Oh, Doll," I mock her. "If people could see the difference between the public you and the private you." I turn the knife around in my hand and grab it in the tiny space just between the handle and the blade. "You just love being a bad bitch in front of everyone, don't you?"

I drag the handle against her inner thigh. From her knee all the way to the apex of her thigh. I use two fingers to spread her lips, smear the handle with the blood on her abdomen and bring it to her clit.

"Shit," she moans. "Rach...Rach I need this."

"You've got your own little fan club, you've got everyone at your feet." Jealousy rises in me, and my little demon takes over the angel that usually rests on my shoulders. "You love fucking other bitches and then parading me around like I can't escape you," I growl. But it's not me. I promise it's not me, it's the devil that has taken my soul.

I let her rub herself against the handle until she's close to coming, until her moans get higher, until her breathing is all over the place. And then I take it away.

"No," she whimpers. "Please..."

"God, if they could all see you now," I snicker. I put the now bloody handle at her entrance and watch as her wet pussy desperately tries to swallow it. But I don't let her, I keep it in the exact same place, I don't move it an inch. "Rose White, the queen of broken hearts, panting like a bitch in need for me."

She nods, her features twisted with need. She keeps trying to lower herself to push the handle inside her, but every time, I move it a little, not letting her get what she needs.

"Look at me," I order low. Her night blue eyes snap open. They're black from her dilated pupils. "You're going to keep your eyes on me while you fuck yourself on that knife like the desperate slut you are."

Hesitation flashes in her eyes for about two seconds before she nods. She needs to orgasm too badly to refuse me anything at this point.

"Do it." I smile, and it must look like a horror show. With fake blood and her blood around my lips, with my makeup probably running down my face, a red contact in my eye. She must love it. "Make yourself come, dirty doll."

She lowers herself onto the thick handle, her eyes on me and mine on hers. I drink in the moment the pleasure overwhelms her. I lick my lips when her moans grow loud again. My gaze darts low and I watch as she moves her hips and forces the handle in and out of her needy pussy. She's soaking, it's bloody, the handle appears and disappears in and out of her in such hotness, my own pussy drips with need.

Keeping the knife tight against her, I take off my thong and move so I can be by her side rather than between her legs. I watch her whole body with passion. The way her toes curl into the sheets, the way her heels push against the mattress to help her movement. Her calves are tensed, her thin thighs are shaking. I can see the tendons at the apex of her thighs stretching to accommodate her open legs. Her slim waist is going from side to side as she circles around the handle, her small boobs are flattened from the position, but they still move to her rhythm.

And her lips... she's biting her plump bottom lip so hard I'm surprised it's not bleeding.

Her eyes, they're mesmerizing. The blue is so dark, so greedy, it's searching for my soul. It wants to suck on it.

I softly grab her hand, peeling her slim fingers off the sheets. Our eyes are locked together but I don't need to watch to know that she's already stretching out her fingers to welcome me. I grip her wrist tightly and sink onto her hand. My wetness welcomes her. She flicks her wrist, her arm tensing. She keeps fucking herself, and at the same time she fucks me. She fucks me relentlessly. And I help her. I sink onto her, I rise and fall, keeping her hand tight against me. I give her everything I have. I clench around her, I pinch her nipples as her screams get louder and mix with my moans.

When we come, our eyes are still on each other. We're both dying to squeeze them shut, but the torture of obliging each other to look is blissful. She forces herself on the knife so hard, my hand slips and I get cut onto the blade. I wince and my pussy tightens around her fingers as I come. It makes both of us groan harder.

I come so hard, the whole room disappears as I fall against her. But I force myself to recover. I push myself up and slide between her legs again as I slide the knife handle out of her. I'm quick to bring it to her mouth and watch her take it between her lips like the queen she is. She licks her blood and her juices with her skilled tongue. She makes me wish I was the handle as she takes it all in her mouth and her cheeks hollow around it.

I bring my head down and lick all of her pussy. I spread her lips and lick her clit, slit, her wet hole that's already tightening again. I lick the blood, the wetness, the mess that she's made.

"Dirty doll," I pant in-between licks. "Dirty, dirty, doll."

71

She moans around the handle, and it makes me go insane. I bite into her thigh, I bite her clit and rejoice at her scream. I take her lips in my mouth, suck them until I own every single part of her. I come back up, crash my lips against her mouth and share the copper and sweet taste with her. We dirty our mouths, lick each other's tongue and clash our teeth in a disgusting kiss that makes me wet again.

When we're done. We're both panting, our hearts racing to match the madness that just overcame the both of us.

"I love you," she whispers in-between two pants.

My heart soars. It somersaults in my chest like a cheerleader tumbling at a competition. It jumps high enough to reach the sky, grab onto stars and bring them back into my belly.

And just like that, with the three rarest words that ever pass her lips, the demon fades away, and the angel on my shoulder comes back quietly...peacefully. Like nothing happened.

CHAPTER 7

Pussy is God – King Princess

Rose

Something stirs beside me, waking me up from a light sleep. Rachel is slipping out of bed.

Shit, I fell asleep after sex. Again. I'm lying on my stomach, my arms at my sides, okay so it must have been a deeper sleep than I thought. It feels like we had sex two minutes ago but when I look at the clock on my nightstand, it's 4:50 am. Damn, I slept. I look down at my body, only now realizing Rachel dressed me in the large sweater I wear as pajamas. Wow, I was *out* out. Orgasms are so fucking tiring.

I don't move, I just watch her take off her summer dress with sleepy eyes. My gaze takes in her beautiful body. Her skin is a porcelain white, and I instinctively lick my lips when her dusty pink nipples harden at the cold.

I let out a needy groan when the dress drops to the floor, exposing her beautiful pussy. Fuck, I love Rachel's pussy. Unlike me, she keeps a thick line of hair that hides her lips and goes all the way up. It's beautiful, so tempting.

Her eyes snap to me when she hears me. She thought I was still sleeping.

"Awake?" she smiles.

"Uh huh. Why are you silently begging to get fucked?" I grumble in a sleepy voice.

She giggles softly. "I'm just getting out of my costume." She grabs one of my t-shirts hanging on the back of a chair and slips it on.

Fucking fuck, that shit looks so hot on her. It's just a black t-shirt. It's a simple black t-shirt that is a bit too big for her. I always have to buy from the tall section if I don't want to look like I'm wearing children's clothes, and she looks like the sweet baby girl she is in it.

"I'm gonna have a quick shower, I'll be back."

She looks so angelic right now. That little demon in her is satiated and gone for now.

She opens the door, steps out and-

My heart drops in my stomach when she closes the door behind. I jump out of bed so suddenly the room spins. My blood rushes to my head, my stomach twists in sickness and I run to the door.

I stumble in the rush, my breath caught in my lung, my body already suffocating from fear. I grab the handle fast and hard, violently opening the door, and breathe in the air outside of my room.

It wasn't locked.

It's not locked.

I'm not stuck.

Rachel hasn't even had time to make it to the bathroom. She turns around and gasps when she sees me.

"Oh my god," she whispers in panic. "I'm so sorry, I'm so... Rose."

She runs back to me, putting both her palms on my cheeks.

"Are you okay? I'm so tired, I didn't even think." Her breathing is just as fast as mine now. The apology in her eyes is real.

"It's okay," I try to say. I take a few seconds to catch my breath, to force my brain to understand there is no danger. "I'm fine," I finally smile.

"I'm sorry," she repeats.

"It's nothing," I reassure her.

"No it's not nothing. I know, I know not to close your door if you're on your own."

I shake my head and grab her hands on my cheeks. I kiss one after the other and release them at her side. "I'm fine, Sunshine."

She can sense my usual confidence coming back, the half-smile, the image of invincibility that everyone believes blindly.

"Go wash yourself," I nudge her.

She nods, but she isn't convinced. Yeah, neither am I. She leaves me alone anyway.

I walk back into my bedroom and make sure to leave the door ajar. That's all I need, just that small opening that promises me I'm not locked in. I find my pack of cigarettes and open my window.

I built a reading nook last year and it's become my favorite place to chill. I sit down, light up a cigarette and watch the November rain starting to fall. Fog is spreading around the Murray's backyard and it brings me a sense of comfort. I rub my itchy nostril, let my head fall against the wall, and smoke in silence.

But that's never good, is it? Silence that is.

My brain slowly wakes up, everything in there is clear as day, memories flooding me in perfect illustrations. The complete opposite of that beautiful fog outside. It's thick and confusing. Comforting.

I take another drag, letting the nicotine relax my body. But it doesn't matter, my mind is already working hard at making my life hell.

A door lock. Click. The smell of a cigar, the warm yellow light of the office. The bright red carpet.

Crack.

Does that hurt, Rose? My beautiful flower, tell me it hurts.

The library is full of Italian books.

Scream, Rose. Scream for me.

Se una Notte D'inverno un Viaggiatore.

Pain. I scream.

La Divina Commedia.

That's my good girl.

His favorite collection are all the books that have Rose *in it. It doesn't matter what they're about. He just wants to see that word plastered everywhere around him.*

Il Nome della Rosa

"Rose?"

I startle at Rachel's voice, my cigarette slipping out of my fingers.

"Shit," I mutter. I grab the burning stick right away and take another drag as I watch Rachel come toward me. She's only wearing a towel. Her shoulder-length blonde hair is wet, dripping onto the floor. She's taken the contact out and her blue eyes are calling for my soul.

"You were completely gone," she sighs. "Again."

"Huh...time to busy my mind then," I smirk. I throw the cigarette in the ashtray by my window and walk to her.

I don't give her time to ask any questions, she knows I won't answer. I grab the back of her neck and force my lips on hers. I push hard, making her whimper as she takes a step back to balance herself.

"Why don't you fill my brain with your beautiful moans," I growl low. "Why don't you let me make you feel so good, you won't remember your own fucking name."

"Rose," she mewls as I ravage her mouth. "You should rest."

It makes me laugh. "I'll rest once I've eaten that gorgeous pussy of yours."

I push her against my desk and raise one of her legs until her foot is resting on the chair. I drop to my knees and push the towel up. "Mm," I lick my lips. "All clean, just for me."

"All clean so we can rest and..."

She doesn't get to finish her sentence. My tongue is flat against her slit and she gasps.

"And?" I ask.

"And..."

This time, I harden and point my tongue until it passes her lips and reaches her wet hole. I drag it until I'm licking her clit.

"And?" I insist.

"Fuck..." she moans. She grabs my hair and rocks against my tongue.

My phone rings somewhere in the room and Rachel's grip tightens.

"You better not take that," she moans as she grinds against my face some more.

I pull back slightly. "That's the guys' ringtone."

Yeah, Jake and Chris have special ringtones. That's so I know

77

if I should ignore it or not. I'm more likely to pick up when I know it'll end up in an argument if I don't. I shouldn't have put my phone on loud, at least if it was vibrating, I wouldn't know it's one of them.

"Ugh, Rose," she complains as I look around and grab my phone on the floor by the bed.

"The fuck you calling me for?" I snap as I pick up.

"*Chris is worried,*" he replies.

What a surprise. I look at Rachel, with her fuck me eyes and her hand sliding to her slit.

'*Don't,*' I mouth. She better not touch herself.

"I don't think he wants to know what Rach and I have been doing." Hopefully the message is fucking clear.

I can hear him refrain a laugh. "*There's a video of you threatening some big guy on Beth's story. So, Rachel's your girl now?*"

That makes me laugh. Of course he'd get a little dig at me before hanging up. "We have a new agreement," I say as I lick my lips. Watching her wait for me like that is such a fucking turn on. "You should have seen Carlo trying to talk me out of punching that dude's face." I sniff, my body remembering how high I was only a few hours ago.

"*Where are you?*" God he's so annoying, and it won't get any better now that Nate is back.

"That door across the hall from yours, that's my room." Duh.

Rachel moans a complaint and stomps her foot like a brat.

Jake must hear it because he finally gives up. "*Have fun coming down tomorrow,*" he concludes.

Not being able to help myself, I throw one last mocking commentary at my twin. "Make sure Jamie grabs her clothes back from the living room before I get out of bed. We share that sofa, Jake. That's nasty."

78

He hangs up and Rachel doesn't wait one second. "Rose!"

"You're about to get fucked for that bratty behavior," I snap at her. I'm not even angry, I just want to fuck the hell out of her.

"Yeah?" she taunts as she walks toward me. Her hips sway, her back arches slightly and she stops right in front of the bed. "Are you going to fuck me hard? Are you going to teach that little brat a lesson?"

I used to wonder how Rach and I can switch so easily. One minute she's cutting into my skin and calling me her doll, the next she begs me to correct her bratty behavior. Then I realized we're just a perfect balance.

No wonder I'm so fucking in love with her.

"On the bed, on your back," I order. She bites her lip, looks me up and down, and hurries into position. "Atta girl."

I open the bench and grab what I know will make our night. I turn it on, and she doesn't need to look down, the buzzing sound is already making her smile.

"Mm...you look way too fucking happy," I tell her.

She pouts and I get on the bed, right on top of her. I kiss her animalistically. I suck on her lips, on her tongue. I lick the roof of her mouth and share the lust I have for her. She is so responsive when I'm topping her, it's like she was meant to be under me.

I pull back slightly and tease her nipples with the vibrator. She brings her own hands to my breasts, and I tut her. "Above your head."

She keeps feeling me and as much as it feels amazing, this is not the game we're playing right now. "Now, Sunshine," I growl.

She finally executes as she starts writhing under the vibrator. I don't push, I just keep teasing her nipples, one after the other. I lean down slightly and grab her wrists in one hand as I keep them above her head.

"Little bratty slut," I rasp in her ear. I lick her earlobe, I trace her neck with my tongue and suck until I know I've left a few hickeys as a present. I lick her lips and she opens for me. She moans into my mouth and my whole body shivers.

I shift so I'm straddling one of her legs and let her feel how wet she's making me.

"Oh god," she moans. "Rose...you're so wet."

"That's your fault."

I bring the vibrator down slowly. I watch as her beautiful stomach tenses under the vibrations, how she shifts and lets out small begging sounds. She instinctively tries to rub her thighs, but she can't while I'm straddling her leg.

I bring the vibrator to the apex of her thigh, I touch her mound, I go around her pussy, never touching the place she desires the most.

She squirms and whimpers, she bucks her hips and every time her thighs tense it hardens against my clit. I rub against her, making myself moan as I stop her from getting any pleasure.

"Please," she whispers.

"Mm...that word, Sunshine. It's a gift coming from your mouth."

I moan again as the pleasure from grinding against her thigh becomes blissful.

I let go of her wrists just long enough to spread her lips and put the vibrator against her clit, she bucks instinctively, and a loud moan escapes her lips. I grab her wrists again and lower the intensity.

"No, no, no," she whines as she grinds against the toy.

"Oh no," I pout. "How are you gonna get satisfied now?"

"Please," she groans. "Rose, baby, please."

It makes me laugh. "You're so pathetic."

"I know," she cries out.

"Such a filthy slut," I insist. "Mine."

"Yes!"

"Say it."

"I'm your filthy slut! Please, Rose!"

I press the vibrator harder against her clit, and the next second I put the intensity to max.

She explodes against it, crying her release and bucking off the bed. I hold her wrists tighter and before she can come down, I straddle her whole body. I press myself against the vibrator and look down at her.

I moan as the vibrations travel from my clit and through my whole body. I rock against the toy, against her, and her eyes widen.

"I...I can't anymore," she pants.

"You wanted it, now you be a good girl and take it."

"Aah..Rose..."

"That's it," I moan. "Take it..." I lift up slightly, giving myself some respite and avoiding to come too soon. I'm not done with her.

I force another orgasm on her before lowering myself.

She desperately inhales a ragged breath. She's whimpering and tears are springing into her eyes from too much pleasure, but she's finally entering her sluttiest phase and I'm not about to let that go.

"More?" I taunt.

"Noooo," she groans as I press the vibrator harder against her. Her hips shift but she moans loudly. "Fuck...fuck..."

I grind against it and look down at her writhing body. I bend down and kiss her before pulling away just slightly. "Open wide," I growl. "Stick out your tongue."

She executes quickly.

"Following orders like a good little bitch," I smile. "Wider."

She stretches her lips, sticks out her tongue far and flat, and I smirk with all my smugness before spitting in her mouth.

She moans from the action and swallows before re-opening.

"Good girl," I gloat. I kiss her open mouth and do it again. I spit in her mouth and watch her swallow. And I come.

Fuck I come so hard I see stars. She follows, and we rub our needy bodies against the other, against the vibrator. We kiss each other until we run out of breath. We lick each other's nipples. I pinch and I bite her, leaving my mark all over her body. I force another orgasm out of her with my fingers and I ride her face until she's drinking me.

We're hungry, possessed. We can't get enough of each other. Never. I want to stay like this forever. I want to use her, abuse her. I want to offer her my body like a faithful worshipper. I want her to mark me as hers until the end of time.

When we fall asleep, I'm holding her tight against my chest. She lulls me into a deep sleep with her scent of chamomile and honey. Her soft arm is wrapped around my waist, one of her legs is hooked around mine.

Pure. Bliss.

CHAPTER 8

Not Enough – Elvis Drew, Avivian

Rachel

It's so peaceful to watch Rose sleep. She's a strong woman, that's undeniable. But when she's asleep like this, her features relaxed, her ink-black hair spread around her, it shows how breakable she is.

So breakable.

I'm lying on my side, propped on my elbow and watching her entirely naked body. She always ends up sleeping on her stomach. Even if she falls asleep on her back, she'll twist and turn until she's on her stomach, her soft cheek pressed against the mattress and her arms by her side.

She looks so young, so beautiful, so complete. She looks like someone who is going to wake up and be at peace with herself, with the world around her.

She looks like a child that has the world to discover.

And yet when, around 10 am, she slowly opens her eyes, the darkness of life reflects in the deep blue ocean. So much pain.

What was it, Rose?

You can tell me anything. You can open up. I will always be there for you.

She never does. I hate asking her and I try to limit my attempts to the times where she truly gets lost in the past.

But how will she ever let go if she just keeps trying to bury her trauma?

She thinks I don't know the words she says in her sleep. She thinks I don't know that she never ties her hair up because she hides the letters on her neck that have been burnt into her skin. She knows I'm observant, so why does she think I don't notice these things?

She looks at me, smiles, and buries her face where the sheets meet my left breast.

Like this, her left arm is right in my line of sight. All those small tattoos spread around her forearm with a few higher. I love them so much. Every few weeks, a new one appears. I can't wait until her whole sleeve is done, I will kiss every single one of them, every day. Every minute of every second.

My favorite one is the sun she has just before her elbow. She had it before we started dating, but we always laugh that she did it for me. And every time her hoarse voice calls me Sunshine, my eyes automatically dart to that tattoo.

My *least* favorite is that damn X close to her wrist. The one with a crown at the top, a 19 on the left side of the crossing, a 33 on the right and a W at the bottom. I didn't always hate it, but I do now that I've seen it on this guy's neck.

His name is Sam. I've seen them talk, I've seen the texts he sends her. He even talked to me the first week we went back to school. I could tell they knew each other right away.

My stomach twists and she must feel me shift because her

head reappears. God, she is so beautiful. No one should have lashes that long, lips that red, that plump. Her cheekbones are high, her cheeks soft. She shouldn't be allowed to look that good. Because everyone can see it, not just me. *Everyone.*

Sam too.

"Sunshine," she croaks in a tired voice. "What's wrong?"

It's like we share the same heart. If it beats a little too fast, we both feel it.

"Nothin'," I mumble under my breath.

She doesn't probe further, she drops her head again.

The thing with Rose is she hates pointless arguments. I mean, don't we all? She hates them so much she'll avoid them at all cost. Including lying.

To avoid an argument, she'll lie. About where she was or who she was with.

To end an argument, she'll lie. About her feelings or her thoughts.

She'll withhold the truth, she'll change the story, she'll make it so that the other person is forced to drop it.

And if she gets caught? She'll snap.

It's her most toxic trait. And it's not the only one.

"Scratch me" she moans low. Her voice is more than raspy when she wakes up, it's broken, almost inaudible. Sexy as hell.

I don't even have to ask where. I slip my right hand in her hair and scratch her scalp. She's such a sucker for hair scratches, it's unbearable. She's worse than a cat.

As she purrs at the back of her throat to show her appreciation, my thoughts twirl back to Sam.

He's a dangerous man, it doesn't take a degree to understand that. A giant made of muscles, covered in tattoos, and with the aura of a reaper. I only talked to him once, but when Rose caught

85

it, she was absolutely fuming. I had never had that strange effect from a man. I was uncomfortable when he was talking to me, but not because I found him disgusting. It was because his calmness and darkness did something to me. Something *inexplicable.*

Now all I can feel is pure jealousy every time he crosses my mind. I don't like how secretive Rose gets around him. Every time she gets a text from him, she hides her screen, she gets fidgety, and eventually, she disappears.

She's always had a habit of disappearing, but since this guy showed up in September, it's been worse. The worst it's ever been. She's so familiar around him. They share that tattoo and... that other one...

"Is it for him?"

Shit. It just slipped. I was lost in my bitter thoughts. She turns around in a huff.

"Ugh, here we go," she says as she settles on her back and looks up at me. "What is it, Sunshine?"

"What do you mean 'here we go'," I snap. "Do I often ask shit?"

She shrugs, emotionally retreating like she does so well. "Can't say it's *not* often. But go ahead, what is for him? Who's him?"

Zero questions would be too many questions for Rose.

"Sam."

"Come on, Rachel," she sighs. "You say his name like I cheated on you with him or something."

"Did you?"

"Don't ask stupid questions," she replies coldly.

"Okay, then why does it bother you to talk about him?"

"Because I don't like him. He's a dickhead and it puts me in a bad mood. You're smart, you could've guessed that." She pushes the sheets and gets out of bed. She grabs her large, shapeless sweater, that she manages to look sexy in when she puts it on, and I roll my eyes.

I wrap the sheet around me to give me some semblance of equality now that she is dressed.

"Okay, if you don't like him why do you hang out with him? Why do you share a tattoo with him? Two actually."

Her gaze snaps to me and her brows furrow, but she doesn't deny it.

"So that little heart with an 'S' in it is really for him, isn't it? The one on your hip."

"Oh my god," she chuckles. "You've lost it."

"Deny it, go on. Lie to me," I provoke her.

I really shouldn't, she's going to snap and kick me out. She's going to go to someone else for pleasure. Someone who isn't attached and doesn't ask questions. We're not 'together' at the moment, we're not exclusive. It drives me mad with jealousy when I remind myself that. I just want her love, I just want her.

Is she going to go to him when I leave?

"I'm a bit done with this conversation, Rachel. I haven't had enough sleep for a jealous fit."

"I'm so sorry," I say in a sickeningly sweet voice. I fake a pout and shoot daggers at her. "Maybe you should have slept with someone else last night. They would have left by now. Or even better, why didn't you get Jason to fuck you, you guys never even leave the parties for it."

"That's enough," she barks. "I haven't done anything wrong, you're being a jealous little bitch and you're taking it out on me. I haven't betrayed you, I haven't changed anything about us-"

"That's the fucking problem, Rose. You don't want to change anything about us, you're happy with what we have because

87

it benefits *you*. When was the last time you wondered if I'm hurting from our arrangement?"

"I'm not getting into this now," she huffs again. "This is fucking long..."

"*This* is my fucking feelings," I rage. "Do they matter to you or is it just my pussy?"

She barks a laugh. "Please, if I was only interested in pussy, I would go to someone that does less talking and more fucking."

I gasp in shock, and she closes her eyes, twisting her mouth in regret.

"I'm sorry," she says after a moment of silence. I shake my head and she walks back to me. She settles a knee on the bed as she extends her hand. She puts a strand of my hair behind my ear, but I push her hand away.

"You're such a dick," I fume. I get off the bed, still holding the sheet and start looking for my sleepover bag.

"I'm sorry, Sunshine. I meant, if I wanted something as simple as sex I wouldn't bother with our arguments and our deal and–"

"Stop talking. You're making it worse."

"You started this," she rages. "You basically set up a trap for an argument."

"I *just* wanted to know what's the deal with that Sam guy! I didn't ask you to marry me! God, you're so scared anything I ask is a demand for commitment, you're a fucking joke."

She runs a hand through her hair and pulls at her roots. "I know, I'm sorry, okay? I don't like the guy, he puts me on edge."

"Who is he?"

"Childhood friend. He used to know my old foster dad." Her voice softens and she approaches me where I just went on the other side of the room. "Okay? That's it. I don't know what he's

88

doing in town, but I didn't like my ex foster dad, so I'd rather not be confronted with anyone who knew him." She puts her palm on my cheeks. "That's it," she repeats.

My heart pinches at the mention of her previous foster family, but I still see the lies she's trying to drown in the ocean of her eyes. I've lost her. If she's lying, this conversation is now pointless.

"I'm sorry," I murmur. "I didn't realize that's how you knew him. I..." I sigh and lock my gaze with hers. "You can talk to me," I remind her. "About your previous family, what you've been through."

She chuckles and shakes her head before lying to my face again. "I'm fine, honestly. Don't worry. No more talks of Sam, okay? Let's leave him where he belongs."

"Where?"

"In the past."

I nod and hug her tight, going on my tiptoes and burying my head in the crook of her neck. After a moment of silence, I whisper in her ear, "I want a tattoo with you too."

She pulls away, her eyebrows raised and her arms on my shoulders extended so she can look into my eyes. "You want a tattoo, Sunshine? Is that what's got you in a mood?"

I shrug and smile. "I think it would definitely help getting me in a better mood that's for sure."

"I see," she smiles back. "Get on the bed."

"What?"

"I'll tattoo you."

"You...you know how to?"

"Oh I'm really bad at it, but you never said you wanted a nice one."

The buzzing makes me jump and that makes Rose scoff a laugh.

"Relax," she tells me in her reassuring raspy voice. It's so warm and beautiful. Every time she talks to me, it vibrates in my chest and makes goosebumps run along my skin. "I'm just setting up for now."

I nod but stress is keeping me tense. "I feel a bit exposed like this." Her gaze takes in my naked body.

"I like it," she smiles.

"Maybe I shouldn't do this."

"Maybe you should just relax." She bends over and drops a kiss on my pussy. It makes me giggle, but ultimately it works. I relax.

I watch her insert the needle in the portable gun and set up the ink.

"This really isn't the cleanest conditions," I voice out. "And I can't have it anywhere my parents would see. What are we even tattooing?"

"That's a lot of excuses in a very short time."

"That's a very permanent thing."

She shrugs. "Should we stop?"

I hesitate, my gaze darting around the room. "I don't know."

"You're the one who asked for it, Sunshine."

"Because you and Sam share two tattoos and you share none with me. You're gonna do me, and then I want you to get something of mine on your skin."

She shrugs. She should tell me that I shouldn't get a tattoo out of jealousy. That this is crazy and she loves me whether we share a tattoo or not.

But our relationship isn't healthy like that. No, Rose is a toxic, manipulative bitch and she's not about to stop me from letting her mark me as hers. She loves it, I can see it in her eyes.

I gulp before asking, "Does he have a heart with an R in it?"

She shakes her head, letting out a mocking chuckle. "God, you're so jealous."

"Does he?"

"Yeah, Sunshine. He does."

"Then I want a tattoo of you."

"Okay. Lay back down, you're all tense right now."

I nod and lay back down.

"Tell me I don't need to do it, Rose...to belong to you."

She ignores my request. "Can I choose what it is?"

I sigh. I'm too in love with her, too attached. Too hung up on what we could potentially be. "Yeah," I reply in a shaky voice.

"And where it is?"

I nod silently before adding, "Can I see what it feels like without ink before?"

The vibrating resonates in the room again. "Nah, you'll be fine." She doesn't bother agreeing, she knows whatever she does I will accept it.

A small whimper escapes my lips when I feel the first sting of the needle against the apex of my thigh.

It takes about twenty minutes for her to tattoo me. I keep my eyes shut, daydreaming about how happy we are going to be outside of Stoneview. How I will follow her wherever she goes, because that's how much I love her.

"It's done," she suddenly rasps in my ear. I didn't even realize the buzzing stopped. My skin feels numb on the area she tattooed me.

I open my eyes and go to prop myself on my elbows, but she wraps a hand around my throat, keeping me against the bed.

"I want to see."

That's not in her plans. Her other hand comes to my pussy,

and she rubs my clit with her thumb. I moan and she swallows it with her mouth. She kisses me as her fingers enter me and curl to rub against my g-spot. My back arches and my hips lift off the bed to follow the movement.

"Rose," I moan.

She pulls back and smiles down at me. "Pain makes you so wet," she murmurs low. "I love it."

I only nod as she keeps working me. I'm a tensed elastic band eagerly waiting to snap. And when I do...fuck when I do it's magical. She pleasures me until I run out of breath and I'm panting with need for air. When she slides out of me, she sticks her fingers into her mouth and moans around them as she licks my pleasure. She pulls them out with a pop and winks at me.

"Get dressed, we're going for brunch somewhere."

"Oh, can we go to that place in Silver Falls that's got the whole menu named after Brooklyn Nine-Nine's characters?"

She smiles back at me, her eyes lighting up. "Hell yeah, we haven't been in so long, are you gonna get the Pontiac Bandit?"

I nod excitedly, electricity buzzing at the idea of a brunch date with Rose. "It's a stack of *ten* pancakes, Rose. Give me a reason *not* to get it?"

"Hurry then," she winks.

I nod and run to the bathroom to rinse myself. In there, I look down at my thigh. The tattoo is small and so close to where my thigh meets my upper body. It's close enough that my beautician will be waxing over it. I giggle to myself thinking of it...until my heart drops when I understand what she's written.

Property of Rose White.

It's a shaky writing, doesn't even look like hers.

My hands tremble as my heart accelerates. This is insane, this is...*exactly what she believes.* And I go along with it so much, I play into her games so well that it's become true. My entire identity is Rose White and no matter how scary this tattoo looks, it feels good. It feels so good because that means she loves me. In her own fucked up way, Rose loves me, and she belongs to me as much as I belong to her. I want her to get this tattoo on her as well. I want to see *property of Rachel Harris* on her skin.

It's with a spring in my step that I walk back into the room. I find her dressed in her skinny black jeans and a grey tee. She's texting and smiling at her phone.

And I recognize that smile. That *fucking* flirtatious smile. My heart shatters into a million pieces for the nth time in my life. Too many times to count. Too many breaks and arguments and making up.

"You have got to be fucking kidding me," I snap.

She startles as she looks up and puts her phone in her back pocket straight away.

"Get dressed, Sunshine."

"Show me," I order.

"Do you like your tattoo?"

"Show me the fucking phone, Rose!"

She huffs and takes it back out. I extend my hand as she walks toward me in slow motion.

"You're just gonna hurt yourself," she whispers.

"Yeah?" I say as I take it. "Well maybe this time it'll be hard enough that I won't fucking come back."

I open her last conversation and my eyes tear up as I watch the conversation with a girl called Emma.

Emma: I know you're not the kind of girl to call back. Why are we even texting?

Rose: Just trying to prove you wrong, let's go for another round and that'll clear up that it wasn't just a one-night stand. I do own a heart.

No she fucking doesn't.

Emma: lol. Little slut. If...and I mean IF we go for another round, I don't want that guy with us. He didn't make me come, only you did.

The last text from Rose isn't sent yet. 'I can do that again' she typed. I delete it, tears rolling down my face. I type something else and send it right away.

Rose: She's got a girlfriend you stupid bitch. Go fuck someone else.

Three dots appear at the bottom and disappear. I throw the phone on the bed.

"You're a bitch, god you're such a fucking bitch!" I scream.

"I told you not to look." How can she be so calm? How can she not care at all?

"You just *tattooed* me! Is that just what this is, property of Rose White and nothing else? You just...don't you fucking love me?"

"I do."

"Oh my god, stop. Just stop. Love is not just a word, Rose. It's something that has to be proven every day."

"We're not together, you know how this works," she says low. It's like she's got no emotion.

I rub a hand over my face, wiping the tears.

"I hate you," I sob. "You're the worst thing that's ever happened to me."

My limbs feel weak as I put my clothes on. My heart is numb from the pain.

"Let's go for breakfast," she says as she hands me the t-shirt I had brought in my sleepover bag.

I scoff. "If you think I want to do anything with you right now..."

"Rachel, this is how this works, and you know it. This is how I function."

"Then go to Emma! Go fuck her, go tattoo your name on another girl!"

"I would never, this is just for you."

My brain keeps holding on to those little words. When she says she does things for me, when she makes me feel like I'm special.

"Why do I never learn?" I rasp. "Why do I keep coming back to you? Why do I let you hurt me?"

"It's not my intention to hurt you, Sunshine."

And the worst thing is, that's true. She doesn't understand that it kills me. She's just in search of the other person that will need her like the air they breathe. She just wants to be indispensable, wanted. And if one abandons her like her parents did? She'll have tons of other ones.

"You're so broken," I whisper. I feel so sorry for her. "You're unfixable."

She nods, the pain flashing in her eyes too real. These are the first words that finally get to her. "I know."

"Please, Rose. All I want is to be enough. Let me be enough. I'll never leave you, I love you too much."

She pauses for a brief moment and then shakes her head.

"I'm sorry."

I pinch my lips to try and not throw more insults at her. It's me, my fault. I shouldn't have let her get close again.

"I need to go," I say in a weak voice.

"I understand, I won't stop you."

But she *doesn't* understand. Because if she did, she'd know all I want from her right now is to stop me. To grab my arm and keep me here and tell me she would rather die than lose me.

She doesn't. She walks me through the door. She double-checks I don't want breakfast like this is the most important thing right now. She walks me outside and we wait in silence for Marc to pick me up.

She opens the door for me instead of Marc. It annoys me when she pushes my hand away to put my seatbelt on. Why is she pretending to care now?

"I want to see you again."

"I'll think about it," I snap coldly.

"Sunshine..." I hear the plead in her voice. It gives me hope and my eyes lock with hers. There is so much in her eyes that is begging to be let out. So much she wants to say and I know she's forcing back down her throat. "...make sure to keep your tattoo moisturized. Wouldn't want that *property of Rose White* to fade away or anything."

She drops a kiss on my forehead and steps away to close the door.

Marc leaves and my head drops against the headrest.

It takes the whole ride to my house before she texts me. She doesn't usually do that, she normally leaves it, keeps herself busy with someone else until she's dying for me to give her attention.

Rose: I'm so fucking dumb.

I ignore it.

Rose: I shouldn't have let you escape. You're mine, why did I let you leave while we're angry at each other?

My phone rings but I cancel her call.

Rose: Sunshine...answer me. I'm sorry.

Rose: Please...

She calls. I decline.

Rose: Pick the fuck up. Or I swear I'm coming over, tying you to your bed, and edging you until you're a crying, soppy mess begging to come. Then I'll leave.

My pussy clenches. Shit, don't let her get to you, Rachel.

She calls again and I pick up, cursing myself for being such a stupid girl.

"God, you're so desperate for my attention, aren't you?" I snap at her.

"*I just had a fucking flash of you going to another girl's house right now.*"

"What? Whose house?"

"*I don't fucking know. Some girl you're gonna try to replace me with.*"

I shake my head at her stupidity and unrealistic imagination. Still, I don't say anything. So what if she gets a little worked up?

"*I want to be with you, Sunshine. Just you and me, please.*"

"Until when?" I spit through gritted teeth.

"*Until you're so sick of me loving you, and spoiling you, and punishing the little bratty slut hiding in you, that you ask me to leave you alone. I won't, of course. I'll never leave you alone.*"

"Why don't you leave me alone now? Maybe I need time to think."

"*Maybe you need a slap to your little clit.*"

"I'm serious, Rose."

"*Fine. Take all the time you need.*" She pauses but I know she's not done. "*Until tonight. I'll be slipping through your window tonight.*"

It makes me chuckle. "God, you're so obsessed with me, don't you have a fan club to attend to your needs?"

"*I do. But I only focus on my biggest groupie. She's the only one that counts.*"

"I'm not part of your stupid drool-over-Rose-White fan club," I growl.

"*Please, Sunshine. You founded it.*"

I roll my eyes even though she can't see me. "Are you serious? About us?"

"*I want you, Rachel. Only you. Please.*"

Until she wants someone else. But for now? It's going to be us, *just* us. I want to hold onto that forever.

"My parents are leaving for the airport at 6 pm. Don't forget the flowers to go with your apology."

"*I would never. Don't forget to wait for me naked with your legs spread.*"

"Deal."

"*Deal.*"

"Rose?"

"*Yeah, Sunshine?*"

"I love you, you know that right? I'll never abandon you for someone else," I tell her softly.

She stays quiet for so long I have to check my screen to make sure we haven't disconnected.

"*I can only hope you won't.*" She hangs up.

No 'I love you' back. She called to apologize, we're together. I can't expect too many miracles in one day.

Sometimes, I wonder if Rose is real. I watch the way she makes love to me, I feel every inch of her skin when she fucks me. I drink her up, I share her pain. I see sides of her no one sees, I see a beauty no one experiences. Someone so beautiful yet so broken.

Broken people break hearts.

And I wonder...how many hearts will she have to break before she gives me hers?

AFTERWORD

Shit is about to get real. So hold on.

Thank you for reading this FF novella, the first I share with the world.

I simply cannot believe how far I've made it into accepting who I am and living with myself in my beautiful entirety. I am not the same person I was ten years ago, writing FF fictions in secret in my bedroom, and yet, I am so her.

It's difficult to express into words how important it was for me to write this story, how difficult it was to understand myself when I fell in love with a girl for the first time. I was 15 and it took me a while to understand. A lot of watching The L Word and listening to Tegan and Sara, and discovering what society had tried to hide from me.

I was scared, I handled it my way, I got pointed at, mocked, and threatened. I now know deep down it didn't matter because I was me, period. I didn't realise that back then. I hid myself with shame and pushed someone I loved away because of fear. To this day, I regret that so deeply.

Following understanding I was attracted to women, it then took me a couple of years to understand I was ALSO attracted to men. Oh, how I have grown up now. I took the experiences life offered me, fell in love, got my heart broken, and am now peacefully enjoying my life as a bisexual. It feels good to say.

Now listen to me carefully, people everywhere will try to put you in boxes and label you. Not only straight people, you have to know that you can experience dickheads in every way, shape and form. At the end of the day, what is important is knowing who you are and who matters to you. That is all that counts. You.

Never stop discovering yourself, never stop learning.

Lots of Love,

Lola

ACKNOWLEDGEMENT

It takes many people to put my books into the world, but I always start with my maman and papa. She is the one that has always pushed me to let my imagination lead me, and he is the one who puts the confidence and strength in me to put myself out in this world...even if I never want them to read my books.

Thank you my King for always supporting me and loving me through everything.

Thank you to every single reader who gave this novella a chance. I hope you enjoyed yourself.

Thank you to the readers who have been following me since Giving In. Giving Up is coming next and I can only hope it will be what you all deserve.

Thank you to my Alpha, Lauren, for being the first external eyes on my stories and always helping me turn them into something more. For pushing me and being the most detail-orientated person on this planet.

Thank you to the amazing betas who helped me on this! Laura, thank you for your kind words, encouragement, and for answering all my questions. A special thank you to the two new betas for giving my story a chance having never read anything from me before:

Sinéad, you're awesome and such an amazing person to work with, thank you. Tasha, at this point I'm probably going to have to force you to beta read every single thing I write. Thank you for your encouragement and your help to make this story what it is now. How is one meant to survive without your voice notes?

And of course, thanks to my PA Julia for your precious help! I am so lost without you.

Always, thank you to my family for putting up with me ignoring you while I write and for always checking how the books are doing. They're doing great actually, I love you.

Also by Lola King

Want to know more about Rose's twin, Jake, and Jamie Williams?

Giving In and **Giving Away** are available on KU!

Giving In blurb:

Jamie

Jake White is our king.

A king with a crown of thorns, a heart of stone, and evil in his soul. He hides it well though, under a beautiful smile and eyes that ravage your heart.

But Stoneview Prep's golden boy has always had a dark aura around him. Like a well-guarded secret. A blackness that he never lets anyone see.

"Curiosity killed the cat, Jamie." My mom always tells me.

She never said it would get me in more trouble than I could handle. She never said it would throw me into the dark world of Jake White. And when I not-so-accidentally find out part of Jake's past, I finally learn the consequences of mischievous nosiness.

Curiosity doesn't kill this cat. It turns it into a mouse to be played with.

At least that's what Jake decided.

Jake

Three years. That's how much my twin and I got of freedom before our past caught up with us.

We were doing well, we were being good, we were keeping out of trouble. Most of all, I was in control.

But trouble always finds a reason to make its way back to us. And when it does, Jamie Williams is here to witness it.

In the morning I learned of her existence, in the afternoon she was spying on me like a fangirl.

This girl is desperate to find out what's behind the golden boy's facade I was kind enough to put on.

So be it.

I have time on my hands, darkness on my mind, and a hundred ways to make Jamie Williams bend to my will.

Printed in Great Britain
by Amazon

57377381R00067